SERVE
THE
PEOPLE!

YAN LIANKE

TRANSLATED BY JULIA LOVELL

BLACK CAT
A PAPERBACK ORIGINAL IMPRINT OF GROVE / ATLANTIC, INC.

The translator would like to thank Christopher Rea for his
contribution in bringing Yan Lianke's work to the attention
of the British and Australian publishers, and also for the
assistance that his own translation of *Serve the People!* provided
in resolving linguistic queries while working on the novel.

First published in Great Britain in 2007 by Constable,
an imprint of Constable & Robinson

ISBN-10: 0-8021-7044-7
ISBN-13: 978-0-8021-7044-6

Black Cat
a paperback original imprint of Grove/Atlantic, Inc.
841 Broadway
New York, NY 10003
Distributed by Publishers Group West
www.groveatlantic.com
08 09 10 11 12   10 9 8 7 6 5 4 3 2 1

SERVE

THE

PEOPLE!

THE NOVEL IS THE ONLY place for a great many of life's truths. Because it is only in fiction that certain facts can be held up to the light.

The novel it is, then, for this particular truth.

The story I'm about to tell, you see, bears some resemblance to real characters and events.

Or—if I may put it this way: life has imitated art, re-rehearsing the plot of *Serve the People!*

★

Wu Dawang, Sergeant of the Catering Squad, now General Orderly for the Division Commander and his wife, stood in the doorway to the kitchen, a bunch of pak choi in hand, acknowledging a devastating new presence in the room. The wooden sign ordering its beholder, in bright red letters, to 'Serve the People!' had moved from its usual place on the dining table and on to the kitchen work top. To the left of the exhortation, five stars gleamed; to the right, a water canteen dangled from a rifle while a luxuriant row of wheat bristled beneath.

The pride of the entire division, an exemplar, a model of political correctness, the Sergeant enjoyed an extraordinarily well-developed understanding of the sign's symbolic language. The five stars (the Revolution) together with the rifle and canteen (the Party's history of armed struggle) were reminders of the long, arduous path to Revolution. The wheat pointed to the glorious future: of glorious harvests in the glorious times to come once Communism had been realized.

This sign, its letters burning scarlet against a whitewashed background, its stars, rifle, canteen and wheat emblazoned in red and yellow, had come home one day with the Division Commander. He had gazed solemnly at Wu Dawang as he laid it on the table. 'Do you know what this sign means?' he asked, while his General Orderly set down dishes of food before him.

After a long, hard look, Wu Dawang produced a careful critique.

'Good,' declared the Commander, his face brightening slowly into a smile. 'Very good, in fact—much better than them.'

Though Wu Dawang didn't know who the Division Commander meant by 'them', he did know, and better than most, the People's Liberation Army's three rules of thumb—Don't Say What You Shouldn't Say, Don't Ask What You Shouldn't Ask, Don't Do What You Shouldn't Do. He therefore went back to the kitchen to prepare soup for the Commander and his wife. And from that moment on, the sign became the most distinguished, most illustrious resident of the dining table, casting its mighty symbolic shadow over the lowly bottles of vinegar, chilli sauce and sesame oil.

The days passed, one after another, as time trickled peacefully, indeterminately through the barracks. Every day at dawn, before reveille, the Commander would come downstairs, immaculately uniformed, and set out for the parade ground—for his daily round of drills, and yet more drills. Every night, long after lights-out, he would return home exhausted, take off his uniform, wash his face, brush his teeth and climb upstairs to bed. Revolution and work were the epicentre of the Commander's life, dominating his entire being. Since earliest boyhood, he had held up the Great Events in Our Nation's History — the Sino-Japanese War, Land Reform, the Fight for Liberation — as a yardstick against which to measure the significance of his every day of existence. Even now, on the wrong side of fifty and gazing down the slope to old age, he still relied on the same gauge to calibrate the meaning of his life.

His young, pretty wife Liu Lian, by contrast, led a much less meaningful life. A nurse by training, and seventeen or eighteen years his junior, she hadn't set foot in a hospital since her marriage. No one knew whether she'd given up work voluntarily, or because her husband had wanted her to, but for a full five years now she had stayed at home, ruling this senior officer's roost, keeping company only with the four walls around her and the prestige of their master.

Of Liu Lian, Wu Dawang knew next to nothing. Before he'd taken up his present post, he'd known nothing at all. He had no idea where she'd grown up or when she'd joined the army as a nurse. He didn't know she hadn't worked for five years or, apart from mealtimes, what she did upstairs all day. He didn't know whether the army still paid her salary even though she didn't turn up to work; whether she was from a military family; whether she'd forgotten army protocol in the years she'd been out of uniform. To him, her personal history was a gigantic blank, a mountain range shrouded in impenetrable mist. Beneath the blankets of cloud, the peaks might have been desolate crags emerging from ravines, or carpets of green serenaded by songbirds and festooned with gorgeous flowers and gurgling brooks; but Wu Dawang had no way of telling.

Because these were matters of which he knew nothing, he paid them no attention; and because he paid them no attention, the Division Commander delighted in his choice of orderly. Even though Wu Dawang was a veteran revolutionary of several years' service, even though his personal file was piled vertiginously high with honours, despite all his commendations, awards and citations, despite the fact that twice a year the brigade's Head of Management would name him Model Soldier as unhesitatingly as one would hand a narcoleptic a pillow, still he wanted more—much, much more. Wu Dawang was, in short, a man greedy for laurels, an exceptional soldier fixated on promotion. And it was after one particularly exhilarating performance at a Mass Theory and Practice of Frontline Logistics Competition — in which Wu had recited, word-perfect, 286 quotations and three classic essays ('Serve the People', 'Commemorating Norman Bethune' and 'The Foolish Old Man who Moved the Mountains') by Chairman Mao; had dug a stove, chopped ingredients and presented an immaculate gourmet banquet of four dishes and a soup all within thirty minutes; and had, yet again, been lauded up and down the barracks ranks as Model Soldier — that the Division Commander had selected him as his full-time orderly and cook.

'What is it you must always remember,' the Head of Management had asked, 'when you start work for the Commander?'

'Don't ask what I shouldn't ask, don't do what I shouldn't do, don't say what I shouldn't say,' he replied.

'And?'

'To serve the Division Commander is to Serve the People.'

'More important even than that,' the Head of Management added, 'you must mean what you say, unite theory with practice, and make sure your actions speak as loud as your words.'

'Please reassure the Commander that I will speak as I think, and act as I speak, that I will be both Red and Expert.'

'Excellent,' the Head of Management said. 'Off you go then, and I'm sure more accolades will come your way soon.'

And with that, Wu Dawang was transferred to the Division Commander's own household.

For the past six months, he had stuck cautiously, conscientiously, scrupulously to his brief: he had cooked, grown vegetables, kept the floor and the front yard spotless, tended the herbaceous borders and pruned the trees regularly. After a short spell of home leave, he'd barely left his new place of work — Number One in the senior officers' compound — this whole time. Because of Wu Dawang's tireless dedication to duty, and because of the Division Commander's almost obsessive zeal for the tasks of the Revolution and of the Party, during a recent, centrally orchestrated Streamline-and-Regroup Initiative, the Commander had set an example for everyone by cutting his own household staff to one. This meant that now only two people were left rattling around this Soviet-built military residence once the Commander had gone to work each morning: Liu Lian, the Commander's thirty-two-year-old wife, and Wu Dawang, his twenty-eight-year-old General Orderly—like a single rose and a hoe left abandoned in a vast, bare flower bed.

As to how the whole thing began, Wu Dawang had no idea. He was unaware how many times in the last six months the Commander's wife had looked him over at the dinner table. Or how she had stood at the window, never taking her eyes off him, as he hoed the vegetable patch at the back of the house. He didn't know that, while he'd been pinning back the grapes in the front yard, she'd found herself compelled to draw him closer, magnifying his image through the Commander's telescope, because the vines—as densely fruitful as a Marxist-Leninist-Maoist study meeting—were obscuring her quarry. Over the days and months, she had studied him. Just as a jeweller would scrutinize a diamond or a chunk of agate through an eyeglass, she studied the pearls of sweat on his forehead; like a connoisseur appreciating a piece of rare, purple-threaded jade, she perused the veins in his neck and along his bronzed shoulders. But he—just as a wild pagoda tree is oblivious to the scent of a garden-bound peony—remained insensible, unknowing. Beyond the Division Commander's gated compound, time passed as unstoppably as water flows to the east and the sun sinks in the west. Outside, the furnaces of the Revolution raged, the great rivers rolled and billowed, but within—within, all remained as peaceful as a valley of fragrant peach blossom, of gentle streams and lush, undulating hills, swaddled in a poetic mist of desire.

It was against this idyllic backdrop that, three days ago, as dusk was falling on whichever secret meeting had been scheduled for the second day of the Commander's all-important two-month study-and-discussion conference on streamlining army administration and performance in Beijing, after Wu Dawang had taken dinner with Liu Lian and begun clearing the table, she had sent in his direction a glance beneath whose coolly decorous exterior burned a seething fire. Taking the Serve the People! sign from its place against the wall, she set it down on the mahogany dining table—as lightly, nonchalantly and guilelessly as if she were asking him to fetch something from the yard, or pick something up from the floor.

'Xiao Wu,' she said, tucking the diminutive *xiao* in front of his surname in a casual, blandly affectionate kind of way, 'whenever this sign's not in its usual place, it means I need you upstairs for something.'

Her communication concluded, she knocked the wooden sign meaningfully against the table—a cool, darkly enigmatic sound, like that of jade on agate. Then, just as she did after every meal, she glided sedately up the stairs.

He stood there, dazed, not sure what was next expected of him, a hint of pleasurable disquiet percolating through him. He gazed at her retreating figure as if it belonged to a woman he'd never seen before, following it with his eyes until she turned the bend in the stairs and her shadow disappeared like a tree's evaporating at sundown. He then returned the sign to its proper place, and set about his usual washing of the dishes and other richly revolutionary chores around the house.

★

Even today, that dusk still gleams bright in his memory, the dying sunlight as red as a political slogan freshly daubed across a wall. After Serving the People a respectable while in the kitchen, he went out into the front yard. There he pruned a few superfluous blooms off an extravagantly vigorous bush of scarlet roses, letting them fall into the plastic bucket reserved for the household of the top-ranking officer — even his deputy received only the old-style iron model. After he had watered the other roses and shrubs by the cobbled pathway, the sun finally sank beneath the horizon, taking its vermilion blush away with it to the west. This is the time, on the plains of eastern Henan, when evening cedes peacefully to night, when the voices of the cicadas fade away to almost nothing — the occasional chirruped exception echoed through the barracks like a rousing army chorus, bringing a welcome respite from the eerie quiet. Just beyond the red-lacquered gate of the Division Commander's compound, the footsteps of the relief patrol clattered across the courtyard. Looking up, Wu Dawang recognized a member of his old company, and they exchanged salutes through the reinforced steel gate. He then went back inside the house, still carrying his bucket.

It was at this moment that Liu Lian quietly lit the firebrand of love in her innocently unknowing orderly. He immediately saw that the sign he had returned to its proper home only half an hour ago had been placed, with heart-stopping brazenness, in the middle of the living room, against the bottom of the stairs. Time had begun to wear the stairs' red lacquer into cracks and scars, exposing in places the grain of the wood, which, like the coquettish features of capitalist women in films, now peeped coyly out at the room. Wu Dawang wasted no time: the sign's new position was a silent call to arms more imperative than any barked order. It told him that upstairs there was work for him, and for him alone.

He immediately set down his bucket, as if a command was echoing through the house. But only a few steps up, his mind cast back six months to the day he'd first reported for his new duties. 'You needn't concern yourself with the upstairs,' the Division Commander had said, an understated steeliness to his voice, 'and especially if my wife's not about.' These words now rang in Wu Dawang's ears as deafeningly as if Chairman Mao himself had spoken them, and when he reached the bend in the stairs he slowed and lightened his step—as if the treads were made of glass, barely able to support his weight.

The residual glimmer of the dusk was seeping through the window, like silk gauze washed red and white. A faint yet pervasive scent of decay floated about him. He couldn't tell where it was coming from—the wooden window or door frames per-haps, or the lime cementing the greenish-black bricks—but it was, somehow, curiously feminine. Though he knew perfectly well that it was utterly inappropriate for him to feel now, obeying the sum-mons of his Commander's wife, as he had done on his way to meet his own intended for the first time, still his heart began thumping uncontrollably. This state of agitation, brought on by the prospect of presenting himself before Liu Lian, was unbecom-ing to a revolutionary soldier's dignity and educa-tion, to the lofty emotional and ideological state he aspired to. And so he pulled himself up, thumped his chest and reminded himself severely that he was climbing the stairs because there was work for him at their summit — as if a crucial link in the great chain of Revolution were waiting for him up there, leaving him no choice but to go and retrieve it.

Once he had, with some effort, managed to dam the busy brook of counterrevolution within and calm the beating of his heart, he completed his ascent with a light, steady tread. It didn't take him long to work out that the arrangement of the first floor was precisely the same as the ground: two rooms to the east, a toilet to the south and an extra room facing west. Located directly above the kitchen and dining room, this extra space seemed to be fitted out for conferences, its centre ringed by a circle of wood-framed sofas and tea tables, its walls hung with all manner of administrative and military maps.

This, plainly, was the Division Commander's workroom — like a novelist's study, but a hundred thousand times more important. Wu Dawang blinked at the frenzies of blood-red arrows and multicoloured lines swarming over maps punctuated by brightly scrawled circles, triangles and squares — as if an entire garden had burst into glorious bloom inside the house. He instinctively averted his gaze, suddenly understanding the Commander's warnings about going upstairs. If a man was allowed even a glimpse of the doorway to secrets, those secrets were as good as out. As a soldier, Wu Dawang's sacred mission in life was to keep military secrets secret: to make it his business not to mind what wasn't his business. It was this discretion that had won him the affection and trust of the Commander, his wife, the Revolution and the state.

Once his heartbeat had slowed again, a new, solemn self-possession descended on him. He fixed his gaze on an old-fashioned carved door to his left. Striding over to it, he raised his shoulders and straightened his spine—precisely as any rank-and-file soldier who found himself in the doorway to his Division Commander's office should—tilted his head back, thrust both chest and eyes forward and barked out six over-enunciated syllables: 'Reporting for Duty.'

He was greeted by silence.

Bracing his vocal chords, he barked out a second time: 'Reporting for Duty.'

Silence, like the twilight, continued to wash through the house.

He knew that the Commander and his wife slept in the bedroom in front of him. While working outside, he'd often seen her face at the window, her youthful, aristocratically pallid features poised there, as if frozen within an antique picture frame. Just as the Revolution itself advanced in lopsided paces — now slow, now fast, now inching, now striding — her imprisoned face was sometimes impassive, sometimes animated.

She had to be in there. He'd never known her to call at other houses in the compound, at the homes of the Political Commissar or Deputy Division Commander, or pass the time with their wives. She hardly ever spoke to them, just as the Division Commander hardly ever wasted idle words on his subordinates. This bedroom was the nucleus of her existence, the building around it her whole life. He knew she was in the bedroom and, as he considered trying another 'Reporting for Duty', he instead found himself knocking — twice — on the door. His knuckles rapped against the wood, as on the surface of a drum.

'Come in,' she replied at last. Her voice, low and hoarse, had a narrow tremble to it, as if something — a slight, yielding obstacle — were lodged in her throat.

He pushed the door open. Only then did he see that the light was off, that the room was cast in shadows, the bed, table and chairs melting into partial obscurity. She was seated on the edge of the bed, a book in hand—volume I of *The Selected Works of Mao Zedong*. Later, much later, as he cast his mind back over a memory that had sweetened with age, it would dawn on him that it had been far too dark to read, that she had only been holding the book for show. But at that moment—as it was happening—he had believed she truly was reading, just as he had believed everything else that happened had followed on as naturally and spontaneously as rain falling from an overcast sky, or the sun emerging into a blue one.

'Aunt Liu,' he said, 'what can I do for you?'

'The light cord is stuck,' she replied. 'Would you get it back down for me?'

Following her gaze, he saw that the cord for the light over the bedside table had wrapped itself around its discoloured fitting, and he would need to stand on something to untangle it. So he walked over to her side of the bed, pulled out the chair from under the bedside table, took the woven cane mat off it,

removed his shoes, brushed the soles of his feet—
which were, as it happened, not in the slightest bit
dirty—and laid an old newspaper out on the chair.
He then stepped onto it, unwound the cord and while
he was up there, gave it a tug.

The room was flooded with light.

Against the sudden electric brightness of the interior, the window shone dark, and threadlike
cracks crept, exposed, across the plaster walls. Like
an armoury bereft of exciting, new-issue weapons,
the room held no surprises: a portrait of Chairman
Mao and a framed print of his quotations hung on
the wall, while a plaster bust of the Great Helmsman
kept watch over the writing desk. A large mirror—
its upper edge inscribed with the Chairman's key
imperatives—rested next to a washbowl; to one side
hung the Division Commander's telescope, to the
other the 54-revolver he rarely wore, its leather
holster gleaming dark burgundy. Directly beneath
the mirror was a dressing table, its glassy green surface covered with jars of face cream, pots of face
powder, scissors, combs and other such objects—
luxuries you didn't often see in those days.

None of this, however, confounded Wu Dawang's expectations. Though he'd never before seen the first floor of the Division Commander's house, he had been upstairs in the residence of the Political Commissar and his wife—who worked in the division's accounts office. Their home (another two-storey, Soviet-style construction) was exactly the same as the Commander's: simple, modest, every surface inspirationally resplendent with the glorious traditions of the Revolution. It roused, urged, all visiting subordinates to the most exalted, the most revolutionary homages they could muster—to recount to anyone who would listen the revolutionary past and present of their senior officers, to worship them as idols of political correctness, as lustrous reflections of their glorious Party, as proof positive of the astonishing fortune and honour that had fallen into their laps, permitting them to become soldiers in such a miraculous era.

Wu Dawang was overwhelmed by the hidden, abysslike reservoirs of simplicity lurking upstairs in the Commander's home. As he jumped back down off the chair, he searched for a sentence that would express to Liu Lian his sense of awed respect. He thought of the phrases that rang out most often during New Year house visits in his village: the simplest homes are the most glorious, the most glorious are the most revolutionary; take pride in the traditions of the Revolution, struggle for glory. And so on and so forth. A number of salutations from his military education classes also sprang to mind. For example, the power of tradition can transcend the passage of time to shape our tomorrows. Or, the simplest things are always the most moving, the most moving things are always the simplest. Or (as his Political Instructor had once read out from an editorial), if our leaders can inherit and disseminate the Yan'an Spirit, can embody and pass on the simple virtues of our illustrious Party leadership, our revolutionary endeavours will glow red like the sun, bringing radiant hope wherever they shine.

Intensely moved by the wealth of beauteous expressions that had come so readily to him, he was on the verge of blurting out a few when suddenly he thought better of it. He began to feel that, however impressive they looked written down, if you actually spoke them out loud, they might sound a little indigestible, a little off, like undercooked rice, or sour soup. You might even sound like you were a bit, well, not all there — not quite right in the head. Especially as this was his first time upstairs, the first time he'd been moved by the Yan'an Spirit in Liu Lian's bedroom, the first time he'd wanted to express his admiration to her, he didn't want to regurgitate the pompous formulations found in essays. He wanted to come out with some priceless gems of his own, with the simplest, purest, most moving words he could find.

But the moment he left those fine, worn phrases back where they belonged — in the posters, newspapers, books and deafeningly public broadcasts that were their natural habitat — his head became a vast, echoing cavern, a colossally deserted public square, rudely stripped of its festoons. His face throbbed bright red under the pressure of this inarticulacy, his lips trembling beneath the anxious weight of everything he had on the tip of his tongue but was unable to verbalize.

After removing the newspaper, he put the chair neatly back under the table, replaced his shoes and straightened up, nervous sweat pouring off his face like water from a spring. He listened to the drops hitting the ground, one after another, like rainwater falling from the eaves of a house onto tiled ground below. Finally he managed to garble: 'Is that all, Aunt Liu? If so, I'll be off downstairs.'

'Don't call me Aunt,' she said, sounding irked. 'It makes me sound so old.'

Smiling brightly, he meant to risk looking at her but instead heard himself saying: 'Aunt sounds more — more personal.'

She did not smile back. 'Xiao Wu,' she said, her words heavy with undeclared meaning, her solemnly benevolent expression tinged with a certain nervousness, 'you can keep calling me Aunt in front of the Division Commander and other people, but when there's no one else around, you can call me Sister.'

She spoke softly, affectionately, like a wise old mother counselling a son before he rides off to join the Revolution, or like a real sister taking her little brother to task. Unexpectedly moved, at that precise moment Wu Dawang wanted more than anything else to do as she said, to call her Sister, to seize this beautiful moment and cement their new sibling relationship. To file it, permanently, within the archives of their lives. And yet, Liu Lian was still the Commander's wife, while he was just the General Orderly. Social inequality loomed as insurmountably between the two of them as the Great Wall, their ranks as irreconcilably different as a skyscraper and a hut. Give him superhuman powers, the power to recite flawlessly everything Chairman Mao had ever written, to cook a ten-dish banquet in less than a minute—and still, still that marvellous word, 'Sister', would be unutterable.

Though his lips had stopped trembling, they had instead begun to feel numb or scalded, as if by a sudden mouthful of hot soup. The word 'Sister' died in his throat, killed by cowardice. Overwhelmed by a searing sense of self-loathing at his own failure of nerve, he resolved to look back up at the Division Commander's wife, his new sister and, with his eyes, to communicate his deep, sincere feelings of gratitude and respect.

He slowly raised his head. After a brief, violent explosion somewhere deep inside him, a gorgeous rainbow unfurled before his eyes—a blinding flash of colour that a second, disbelieving look translated, more matter-of-factly, into the Commander's wife.

The light shone bright as day.

The room was so quiet that you could hear the faint buzz of the light waves colliding and merging with solid objects. Outside, a sentry was pacing about the barracks, his footsteps faint but distinct. Wu Dawang stood there, paralysed, as if he were made of wood, without any notion of what he might do next.

Liu Lian, he now registered, had placed the book down on the bed and, as it turned out, was dressed only in a red-and-blue floral silk nightgown which, in the way of nightgowns, hung loose and flimsy on her as if it might tumble off her body at any moment. It occurred vaguely to him that when he had first come in, he hadn't noticed her state of relative undress because the room had been lit only by dusk. Liu Lian, he deduced, must have had the nightgown on all along, but the evening gloom had prevented him from engaging in a thoroughgoing assessment of the situation. Now, with the light back on and an uninterrupted view, the evidence was there before him, clear as day.

Of course, if it had been merely a question of Liu Lian sitting on her bed in a nightgown, he wouldn't have been hallucinating rainbows where his Division Commander's wife was meant to be. After all, he was no longer a boy, no callow member of the rank-and-file, but a man of rank, a squad leader, a married man—he was one of the few guardsmen who'd actually seen a woman. And what a woman! His wife, let it not be forgotten, was the only daughter of a commune accountant. No—it was all the weather's fault. What with it being so hot, Liu Lian had turned on the electric fan at the head of the bed and, every time it rotated in her direction, it dispatched a rippling breeze under the hem of her nightdress which then travelled inexorably upwards to escape via the neckline. The nightdress was roomy enough that each well-aimed flutter of the fan exposed a delicately shimmering, naked expanse of long, slender, snow-white thigh.

In the interests of laying out all the relevant facts, it should probably be made clear that not only was this the first time in his life that the country-born Wu Dawang had seen a woman in a silk nightgown, but also that an enticingly feminine scent of Osmanthus flower was wafting sedately out from under its hem, engulfing every corner of the room, billowing up around him, constricting his breathing. Its oppressive closeness was drawing the sweat from his palms. It left his fingers powerless stumps, hanging uselessly by his sides, trembling as the sweat coursed down them. A single glance at her brought the rainbow flashing painfully back, scorching his eyeballs. But just as he determined to wrest his eyes away, it became apparent once more that the breeze's only logical exit point was the neck of her nightgown.

And there — just one unguarded glance later — entirely at ease within the air-filled nightdress, were her breasts, as flawlessly, geometrically round as if they had been traced with a compass, rising up large and white as the *mantou* — the fluffily perfect bread rolls so dearly beloved of the Division Commander — that he steamed for his superior and his wife. The moment Wu Dawang's mind wandered from the generous display of Liu Lian's bosoms to the steamed rolls he so deftly prepared, his hands registered an impulse to reach out and knead them.

But he was, when all was said and done, a man of education, a man who'd been to middle school, a man in whom the army had planted ideals, a yearning for the higher things in life. He was a man who enjoyed the esteemed regard and confidence of the Division Commander and of the army as a whole, a man who had pledged to fight for Communism until his dying breath. And he knew as well as his own name that he wasn't a son, or nephew, or brother, or cousin in this house—he was just a General Orderly. He knew what he should do and say—and what he shouldn't.

The forces of reason hammered down on his over-heated brain like hailstones, dousing his raging fires with freezing meltwater. The Commander's wife, he reminded himself, was perfectly entitled to wear what-ever she wanted—whatever it happened to reveal—in her own marital bedroom. (Barely a month after their wedding, he recalled, his own wife had taken to strolling around their bedroom naked from the waist up, without a trace of self-consciousness.) Women always remained guilelessly pure of heart in the presence of men, he reflected; it was men with their diseased thoughts who were the problem.

And so it came about that, just as Wu Dawang's soul teetered perilously over a precipice of capital-ist loucheness, the glorious forces of revolutionary reason rushed to its rescue. His gaze slid peacefully over and away from Liu Lian, as an eagle's eyes would skim a still body of water, and came to rest on the volume of *The Selected Works of Mao Zedong* that she had been leafing through. 'Aunt,' he asked again, 'will that be all?'

Displeasure flickering across her face once again, Liu Lian tossed aside the book on which he had fixed his glance. 'Xiao Wu,' she asked icily, 'what must you always remember when working in the Commander's house?'

'Don't say what I shouldn't say,' he responded, 'and don't do what I shouldn't do.'

'And?'

'To serve you and the Division Commander is to Serve the People.'

'Well said—well said.' Relaxing her expression of affront, she pulled her thoroughly aired nightgown back over her thighs. 'Do you know how much older I am than you?' she asked in more kindly, sisterly tones.

'No.'

'Only four years. Still think I'm old enough to be your aunt?' Without waiting for a response, she took a cloth from her bedside and passed it to him.

'Dry yourself off, I'm not going to eat you. Seeing as you can't get it out of your head that I'm your Commander's wife, you'd better answer all my questions—just like you'd answer him.'

He wiped his face with the cloth.

'Are you married?'

'Yes.'

'How long?'

'Three years.'

'Children?'

'We had one the year before last. When I took home leave three months ago, you gave me baby clothes to take back as a present. Don't you remember, Aunt?'

She paused, as if something had suddenly stuck in her throat. After a brief silence, she resumed. 'Stop calling me that: I'm your sister, remember.'

He looked up at her once more.

'What do you want, more than anything else in the world?' she asked.

'To realize Communism—to struggle for Communism until my dying breath.'

She flashed a curious, cold smile—like a thin veneer of embers smouldering over ice. She repeated her question, a harder set to her features: 'I'm your sister, remember, you have to tell me the truth.'

He mumbled a yes.

'So what is it you really want?'

'To become a Party official. To have my family transferred to join me in the city.'

'Do you love your wife?'

'I don't know about love, but when you marry someone you have to look out for them, for the rest of your life.'

'Sounds like love to me.'

A silence fell over the room, as heavy as an army-issue tent. The electric fan was still whirring. Whether it was the heat or his nerves, the sweat kept pouring off Wu Dawang — stinging like seawater when it dripped into his eyes. He knew she was staring at him but for safety's sake he focused only on the *eau de nil* of her bedclothes and the silk mosquito net suspended above. Time limped by as slowly as a decrepit ox pulling a broken cart, until he could stand it no longer. 'Aunt,' he faltered again, 'was there anything else you wanted to know?'

She threw him a cool glance. 'No, nothing else.'

'So, can I go back downstairs then?'

'Yes, all right.'

But just before he reached the safe haven of the doorway, she called him back for one last mystifying question. 'Tell me the truth: do you wash, every night, before bed?'

'Yes,' he replied, baffled. 'When I was a new recruit, the Political Instructor didn't let you get into bed if you hadn't washed.'

'So you wash every day?'

'Every day.'

'You can go now,' she dismissed him. 'But remember: whenever that sign isn't on the table, I want you upstairs.'

He fled quickly down the stairs. As soon as he reached safety, he turned on the kitchen tap and doused his sweat-soaked face in cold water.

BACK IN THE NARRATIVE PRESENT, then, the Serve the People! sign had once more left the dining table, finding its way this time onto the kitchen work top. Before sundown, Wu Dawang had been around the back of the house, watering the pak choi, radishes and chives. As most of his work centred around the kitchen, it was only while he was in the garden that the sign could quietly have slipped out of the dining room to set up ambush in his operational headquarters.

Just as it had done three days ago, the midsummer sunset burned the plains of eastern Henan with a furnacelike intensity. Despite the immoderate warmth of the evening, soldiers were massed in every available space in the barracks—the drill ground, by the sides of roads and thoroughfares, in the yards that fronted company quarters—to practise postprandial drills designed to Oppose Imperialism and the Capitalist Road, and engage in all manner of educational activities aimed at Newly Reconstructing the Superstructure, and Consolidating the Great Wall of Socialism. On the firm ground of the central plains, a glorious revolutionary display was blooming beneath the sultry summer sky.

To the north, the half-dozen residences that housed the division's senior officers lined up in two rows of three, separated from the rest of the barracks by a red-brick enclosure and watched over by sentries and guards—a small-scale homage to Zhongnanhai, the high-walled Politburo compound in Beijing. Each of these six small buildings was further divided from its neighbours by a reinforced steel fence additionally fortified by thick green vines. Each was inhabited by one of the six Supreme and Deputy Commanding Officers, each with his own Personal Orderly. Every day the senior officers would assemble in conference rooms to talk over matters of national import; every evening they would return to their respective residences and refuse to have anything to do with each other. Wu Dawang didn't know why they maintained such splendid out-of-hours isolation. Perhaps they were afraid that fraternizing in private might foster corruption. Perhaps some mysterious explanation lurked deep within the officers' compound or within the larger enclosure of the barracks itself. As none of this was his business, he paid it little thought. All he knew was that to serve the senior officers was to Serve the People.

When he pushed open the kitchen door on his way back in from the vegetable garden, he was holding a bunch of pak choi that he had intended to stir-fry the following morning for Liu Lian. (She was in the habit of eating green vegetables between meals because, she had told him, they were full of vitamins; after meals, she would crack a few pine kernels for the beneficial oils she said they contained.) But the sight of the Serve the People! sign on the work top seemed to have immobilized him—down to his very fingertips, through which the pak choi now slipped, stem by stem, onto the floor by his feet.

Something, he now knew, was about to happen; a course as inevitable as the burning down of a lit fuse had been set. A passionate entanglement lay in wait for him, like a land mine. But knowing it was there was of no help to him in the face of danger; he was uncomfortably aware not only of the landmine itself, but also of the fact that, sooner rather than later, he would have to tread right on it.

He gazed back out through the kitchen door at the garden where a few late sparrows were still skitting back and forth, their merry chirping casting his thoughts into disarray. He couldn't think how to avoid the land mine; all he knew was that it lay in the road before him. And the worst of the whole business was that, even though he knew full well that stepping on it would destroy him, his reputation and prospects, even as he told himself this, a kind of reprehensible, lustful recklessness was willing him onwards—the kind of foolhardy courage that drives a man on toward a tiger-infested mountain, knowing he is likely to be torn to pieces. This intrepid carelessness sowed in him a fearful longing—the nervous, greedy yearning of thieves before a robbery.

As he stood in the centre of the kitchen, staring at the sign, transfixed by anxious anticipation, he thought of the cheerless sexual experiences that he and his wife had shared, after overcoming their ignorance and self-consciousness, in the course of a marriage that time and circumstance had withered into an emotional wasteland.

And yet it was this very landscape — of his blighted marriage — which would set into even greater, more glorious relief the all-consuming passion that was shortly to engulf him, which would serve as the tinny overture to the grand opera into which his affair with Liu Lian would swell.

As the minutes slipped quietly by, the blood-red sun faded to a dull crimson smear and the exuberant sparrows left the garden. A locust was concluding a hazardous trek into the kitchen, reaching Wu Duwang's feet with a final hop. Wrenching his gaze away from the sign, he saw that the insect had clambered, exhausted, onto one of the leaves he'd dropped. As he prepared to gather up the vegetables and flick the locust away, he suddenly became aware that Liu Lian was standing in the doorway to the dining room, as still as a waxwork, a paper fan in her hand, that same loose nightgown draped over her. He immediately acknowledged her presence: 'Aunt Liu.'

She ignored his greeting, her face blanched by an angry pallor.

'I've only just got in from the garden,' he went on. 'I was about to come and see you.'

'You got in ages ago,' she replied. 'You've been standing here at least ten minutes.' Furious, she picked up the sign and banged it hard against the work top. She then spun around and strode back across the dining room, into the sitting room and up the stairs, her soft plastic slippers, fashionable at the time amongst the wives and daughters of well-to-do city families, slapping percussively over the floor. Her anger echoed out from the strident clack of her footsteps. A shiver, then an electric current of panic ran through his entire body. Without another word, he picked up the vegetables from the floor, put them in the sink, hastily washed the mud off his hands and followed her upstairs. He stationed himself in the doorway to her bedroom, head bowed like a scolded child, or a new recruit come to confess a transgression to his commanding officer.

'Sister,' he called out softly.

The instant he'd uttered the word, he marvelled at how easily it had come out; as if without noticing he had said something that would change the course of world events. As Liu Lian sat with her back to the door, in front of the old-fashioned dressing table mirror, it was a change in her countenance—a faint, trembling resurgence of colour—that fully alerted Wu Dawang to what he'd just done. Her face had a slightly dazed look, as if she'd just woken from a dream, while the two curves of her shoulders registered a delicate tremor, like two large apples hanging in the gentlest of breezes. Watching her turn gently around on her stool, he finally became unmistakably aware that those two momentous syllables had slipped out from between his lips. This one word had toppled the Great Wall of hostility that had divided them; it seemed to have set her alight, like a single spark from one edge of a prairie lighting a pile of dry tinder heaped at its other. Wu Dawang contemplated the effect of his utterance, not yet conscious that, like a key inserted into an old iron lock, it had with a single smooth action unlocked the door to love, permitting it to swing gloriously open like the great gate in a besieged fortress.

As Liu Lian raised herself slowly up from her stool, Wu Dawang glanced up at her, then away again.

'Have you washed?' she asked.

'Washed what?' he replied.

'You're covered in sweat.'

He glanced down at his damp work shirt, at the salt marks on his army trousers. Remembering how she'd asked him if he washed every day, how the Political Commissar's orderly had told him that she didn't permit the Division Commander to get into bed without taking a bath first, he started to feel uneasy about introducing the acrid smells of his garden labours into her bedroom sanctuary. 'I wasn't thinking,' he faltered, staring in embarrassment at the sweat stains on his trousers and the crumbs of earth on his shoes. 'I was in too much of a hurry.' Though he spoke in a tone of self-critical apology, a puzzled glint in his eyes inquired as to why, exactly, his personal hygiene should be of such vital import.

She continued to lean against the dressing table, gazing calmly at him, registering though not responding to his bewilderment. 'Put the sign back on the dining table,' she said after a pause, 'then lock the gate, have a shower and come back upstairs.'

He was left no choice but to go back downstairs. 'Plenty of soap!' she shouted out when he was halfway down.

And so he washed.

The Division had taken the unusual measure of installing a showerhead in the Commander's downstairs toilet, under which Wu Dawang was in the habit of giving himself a quick blast whenever he came in from the garden. This time, however, mindful of her intimately explicit instruction, he washed himself all over—first with ordinary vegetable soap, and then a second time with perfumed soap, to guarantee that the results would be both clean and fragrant. He scrubbed himself with speedy but meticulous efficiency, attending to every inch and crevice of his body.

If, with the benefit of hindsight, we subject Wu Dawang's assiduous ablutions to rigorous analysis, we are led inexorably to the audacious conclusion that, from its very beginnings, he was a willing co-conspirator, or at the very least an eager collaborator, in the liaison that was brewing. At the time, however, he remained unconscious of his own complicity. Again and again, the bars of soap slipped out of his trembling grasp, his heart pounding so wildly he almost feared it would gallop out of his chest. Days—many days—later, Liu Lian would still tease him, stroking his head, about how he had rushed back up to her that evening with streaks of soap running through his hair.

Most of his clothes were in his company barracks, but for emergencies he kept a spare white cotton shirt and pair of yellow underpants in a cupboard in the Division Commander's kitchen. While he hastily dressed, inserting his left leg into his right trouser leg, he found himself unable to master his feelings of agitation through the power of reason; a rush of blood to his head had swept away any possibility of rational thought. All he could grasp, dimly, was that Liu Lian was waiting for him upstairs, like a honeyed trap into which he was longing to step. He hungered for her soft skin as a starving beggar hungers for bread; he thirsted for her rosy, round face as a parched throat thirsts for a sweet, ripe melon.

As he showered, fancying that he could still smell her Osmanthus-flower scent, his overwhelming impulse to succumb to temptation had transformed itself into something altogether more noble—into the will to sacrifice everything for love. At that moment, his only desire was to complete his brisk toilette, then charge directly upstairs to discover what exactly it was she wanted of him, what lay behind that enigmatic sign. He wanted to throw open the door to her bedroom and find out everything there was to know there, like a child desperate to explore a mysterious cave he had chanced upon.

He was still dressing as he climbed the stairs, still struggling to do up his buttons as he reached the top. Time has long since blunted the sense of feverish anxiety that took hold of Wu Dawang as he ascended, dulling the memory of his excitement like so much dust collecting over a cherished memento. By now it was dark outside. Through the window on the first-floor landing Wu Duwang could see squares of weak yellow light from the barracks windows. Occasionally, soldiers on night duty could be heard shouting to each other across the parade ground. Approaching the door to her room, he heard her soft, padding footsteps.

She was waiting for him behind that door.

He knocked.

Just then, he noticed he'd buttoned his shirt up wrongly. Hastily undoing, then redoing it, he tugged it down flat. As he smoothed out his trousers, he tried to slow his heartbeat, then stood once more, ramrod straight, in front of the door. Having recovered some semblance of calm, he cleared his throat, as if about to launch into a long dramatic monologue, then announced his arrival with the same solemn declaration as three days ago: 'Reporting for Duty.'

But the words that emerged no longer resonated from within, but were gasped out, weak and hoarse—as understated in their enunciation as any casual, colloquial interjection. He fell silent again, waiting to be beckoned in as before. This time, however, no such instruction floated out. The only sound was of Liu Lian's footsteps quietly retreating into the room, followed by a dry, cracked cough after she'd sat down on the bed.

Although he understood that her cough was precisely the summons he'd been hoping for, he took a step closer in, to make perfectly sure: 'I've showered,' he informed the door. 'What was it you wanted?'

This time he received an answer: 'Come on in.'

And that is how simple the whole business was, skipping blithely over a great mass of plot details and connections. But this is just how things were with this love story—its beginning, middle and end bereft of the intervening complexities one might imagine necessary to an affair of the heart. For complexity does not inevitably heighten a story's verisimilitude, or its power to convince; sometimes simplicity and economy make for a more vigorous exposition, propelling the drama forward.

Wu Dawang opened the door.

When he entered the room, he discovered it was pitch black: sunk in the total darkness of the country nights he'd known before joining the army, a darkness that left you stumbling blindly into the village's deepest wells and along its gloomiest lanes. To Wu Dawang, it felt like tumbling—in an instant—from blazing, surface sunlight down into the impenetrable obscurity of an underground cave.

'Liu Lian,' he quavered, 'Sister,' as though this were an incantation capable of dispelling darkness and bringing light.

'Shut the door.'

Her voice, he judged, had come from the corner of the bed, which meant she was either sitting on the bed itself or on the chair in front of the dressing table. He reached back for the door, and pulled it shut. 'Now come over here,' she continued. Her words had a mysterious traction, dragging him forward at her command. When he was a few inches from the foot of the bed it gave a slight creak, which told him she was sitting neither on its edge, nor on the chair in front of the table, but was lying right in the middle of the mattress. In the great scheme of this seduction, of course, there was no real qualitative difference between Liu Lian occupying the middle or one side of the bed. But at the time, there was something about the discovery of her precise location that stopped Wu Dawang in his tracks. As the sweat ran off him like rain down a pillar, suddenly all he wanted to do was throw open the window and door to let in the cool night breeze. He listened to her breathing — reeling in and out, as smooth and silken as gossamer thread — while his own rasped rough and heavy in great, strenuous gasps.

At this point in proceedings, our love story resembles, perhaps, a steam train halfway up a mountain, each new inch forward demanding an agonizing expenditure of effort. On reaching the peak, of course, the train would regain its momentum and rush exhilaratingly down the other side, through glorious, balmy evening sunshine. But for the time being, Wu Dawang had ground to a halt. He could not explain why he should suddenly find the idea that she was lying naked on the bed so disconcerting. While showering and coming back up the stairs, he had yearned for this as instinctively as dry tinder longs for fire, as fire longs for strong winds. But just as his desire teetered on the edge of realization, timidity barred all further progress.

Time passed, the seconds ticking into minutes, the room still consumed by that irresistible darkness. Wu Dawang mopped his sweat away for a third time.

'Are you all right?' came a gentle voice from the bed.

'Please turn the light on.'

'It's too bright.'

'Please turn it on, I've something I want to say to you.'

She fell silent again, as if the effort of considering his request exhausted her ability to generate sound. Listening to his own breath fall through the air and onto the ground, he even began to hallucinate the physical form of her exhalations on the bed. Oppressed almost beyond endurance, Wu Dawang actually began to fear for his life; death either by suffocation, or from shock was starting to seem a real and frightening possibility. In a last desperate attempt at self-preservation, he repeated his request: 'Please put the light on.'

She continued to pursue the most powerful, most expedient course of action open to her—neither speaking nor moving.

As time dragged on in the warm, velvety blackness, Wu Dawang felt compelled to issue a foolish ultimatum.

'If you don't turn the light on, I'm leaving.'

Again foolishly, he took a step backward.

At the sound of this threatened retreat, she sat bolt upright on the bed, groped for the cord and yanked on the light.

Just as it had done three days previously, one sharp click transformed the darkness into radiance.

Just as it had done three days previously, a flash of coloured light scorched his eyeballs. History was repeating itself: a history of unconsummated passion falling anticlimactically away. When all that he'd expected, all that he'd wanted, did in fact come to pass, he was once again incapacitated by panic.

Sure enough, there she sat, like a jade statue, in the middle of the bed beneath the mosquito net, naked except for a corner of red blanket tugged skimpily across her thighs. To Wu Dawang's surprise, however, as Liu Lian appeared before him under that dazzlingly revealing electric light, her face was suffused by a proud confidence in her own dignity. As she stared defiantly at him, her red silk brassiere — an item of clothing that, back then, Wu Dawang had never heard of, much less seen — hung at the head of the bed, glaring lopsidedly, like a pair of bloodshot eyes. Her breasts maintained an attitude of furious immobility, her nipples jutting forward like the pink noses of two indignant white rabbits, bearing solemn witness to the scene playing out before them. Her hair was draped in a frozen wave over her pale shoulders, resembling, in its perfect stillness, fine black wire.

All impulse for passion had died in her, killed not only by the extinguishing of the seductive darkness, but also by his outrageous persistence in remaining motionless before her. He had surely forgotten that he was her General Orderly and cook, that she was the mistress of the house, the Division Commander's wife, that to serve the Division

Commander and his wife was to Serve the People. Under the burning white lamplight she faced him, the translucence of her skin generating an aura of irreproachable virtue. While he, by contrast, stood staring like a sordid voyeur. Throughout this stalemate, her own clear sense of superiority—apparent in her piercing glare and mocking lips—cast a chill over the room's stuffy interior.

As normality, with all its subdued frigidity, returned, the sweat on Wu Dawang's face dried. She might have been naked, but she was still the Division Commander's wife. He might have been fully dressed, but still—still—he was only the General Orderly and cook.

'Say whatever it is you have to say,' she remarked lightly.

'I'm afraid,' he mumbled into his chest, after a brief hesitation.

'Of who?'

'Of the Division Commander, and of the Party.'

She gave a cold smile. 'So it's only me you're not afraid of?'

When he slowly looked up, he saw that she had been silently scrutinizing him all the while, as one

would examine a utensil. She heaved a long, regretful sigh—the kind that might follow the realization
that an object was not fit for purpose—then twisted
around to gather up the nightgown lying on the bed
and pulled it on.

'You're not worth the mud these walls are made
of,' she finally concluded. 'I expected more of you,
Wu Dawang, I really did.'

MUCH OF WHAT HAPPENED NEXT had more to
do with army protocol than the course of true love.

Wu Dawang spent his whole journey back to
barracks that evening — a half-mile that took him
across the drill ground — worrying whether his
behaviour had been right or wrong. Now that
lights-out had sounded, most companies had turned
in for the night, and a lonely silence was descend-
ing. The moonlight spilled out of the July night sky,
tinging the drill ground dark green beneath its cold
fluorescence. A cool breeze was starting to blow in
from the east, whisking away the scorching heat of
day. A few of the older soldiers had crept out from
their slumbering companies to gather in small soci-
able groups in corners of the deserted drill ground —
to talk and laugh, to have a drink and a song. The
fierce, peppery fumes of their liquor, together with
the strains of their revolutionary choruses, floated

on the wind, quickening the hearts of all those they swept over.

Wu Dawang also decided not to go straight to bed. He wound his way around those companionable clusters of drinkers to the deserted, southernmost end of the ground. There he sat, alone. To any casual observer, this deep moonlight contemplation might have suggested an inquiry into the fundamentals of existence, into the ethics of love, desire and revolution, into the conflict between honour and self-interest, into duty and hierarchy, human nature and animal instinct. But in reality these thorny abstractions slipped by him like smoke, leaving behind only two considerations: one, Liu Lian's extraordinarily seductive body; and two, the probable consequences of entering into the kind of relations that she seemed to be proposing, and the Division Commander finding out. The simple but powerful blade of his mind stripped the issue of all complexity, leaving only these two principal contradictions. Meditating on the former, he was lost in blissful daydreams; thoughts of the latter called up the terrifying presentiment that just around the next corner of his life an execution ground awaited.

On the battlefield, multitudes had met their end at the hands of the Commander—it was common knowledge that during the Civil War, he had blown an enemy's head off at close range before stamping, repeatedly, down on it. Picturing the entire scene to himself—that mangled ball of human flesh trampled beneath the Commander's army boot—Wu Dawang shivered and vowed that Liu Lian would have to shoot him before she had her way with him; he would defend, to the death, his honour as a soldier and a revolutionary.

If my wife didn't have to work in the fields every day, he thought to himself, I bet her skin would be softer and whiter than yours.

If my wife had your clothes and face creams, she'd probably be prettier than you.

If my wife had grown up in the city, she'd speak just as nicely as you.

Sometimes my wife smells just like you or, if she doesn't, it's only because she doesn't have time to bathe as often as you do. Think your soft skin, pink cheeks, big eyes, white teeth, tiny waist, firm breasts, long legs and round buttocks would be enough to turn my head? A revolutionary soldier? And how did a capitalist-bourgeois slut land a war hero like the Division Commander anyway?

When Wu Dawang stood up, except for his sense of perplexed regret about the Commander's choice of mate, he was much lighter of heart. He felt that his simple, honest soldierly virtues had, for the moment, vanquished his would-be seductress. He was filled with pride: pride at his extraordinary ability to scorn the Division beauty, at his own incorruptible integrity. But just as he was about to retire, proudly, to his dormitory, up popped his Political Instructor out of nowhere.

'You certainly know how to make yourself scarce, don't you? I've been looking everywhere for you.'

He studied the Political Instructor's face by the light of the moon.

'Was there something you wanted, Sir?'

The Instructor snorted.

'I expected better of you, Wu Dawang, I really did. I never dreamed that you — you, of all people! — would cause me this kind of trouble. I've just had the Division Commander's wife on the phone, and she was less than happy. She told me you had no idea that to serve the Division Commander and his wife was to Serve the People. She said she wanted you replaced first thing tomorrow with someone new, someone who knew something about political theory. Come on, spit it out, what did you do to her? You're a Sergeant, a Party member, you've got awards and honourable mentions coming out of your ears, there's no one I trust more in the company. How on earth did you manage to forget to Serve the People? Spit it out,' he repeated, 'what was it? Cat got your tongue?

'The Revolution is not a dinner party,' the Instructor continued. 'It's no walk in the park. It's about blood, sweat and sacrifice. Two thirds of the world's population still live in misery and oppression. Under Chiang Kai-shek, the people of Taiwan are suffering from unspeakable poverty, hunger, cold and disease. The People's Liberation Army—that means you and that means me—there's still work for us, plenty of it. The US imperialists are everywhere, our borders are crawling with a million Soviet revisionists. As soldiers, every one of us needs to stand tall and fix his eyes on distant horizons, to think of China and of the world, to keep our feet on the ground and fulfil our duties, to work as hard as we can for the liberation of mankind. But what do I find here? You can't even look after Liu Lian while the Division Commander's away. If you don't look after Liu Lian properly, the Commander won't be able to concentrate on his meetings in Beijing. If the Commander can't concentrate, it'll affect the entire Division's battle training; if an entire Division isn't ready for battle, it affects the army as a whole; and if World War III does break out — then you'll see just how big an influence someone like you and something like this can have. And if it comes to that, a hundred deaths by firing squad will be too good for you. And for me and the Division Commander as well.

'That was the big picture,' the Political Insructor went on. 'Here's the detail. How can you be so stupid, Wu Dawang? I thought you wanted your family transferred to the city, I thought you wanted promotion. A few words from the Division Commander could solve all your problems. And who's going to get these magic words out of him? His wife, the person he sleeps next to. Liu Lian.

'Go to bed,' he finished. 'I'm not going to ask again what it was, exactly, you did. I've agreed to send someone new over tomorrow, as requested. But I've

decided to give you a chance to put things right. So
I'm going to send you back to the Commander's
house for one more day. I'll let Liu Lian know it was
my decision, so if she's looking for someone to blame
I'm her man. But beyond that, it's all down to you.
It's in your hands now. An outstanding soldier is not
content only to take light from the beacon of Revolution, but should also enhance its eternal brilliance
by his own efforts.'

Verbosity—and in military thinking especially—
was the Political Instructor's particular talent. As
his superior held forth unstoppably, Wu Dawang
began to feel a furious hatred for Liu Lian. Several
times he came close to revealing her degenerate,
capitalist attempts at seduction, but each time the
words sprang to his lips he swallowed them back
down, for reasons that were unclear to him. Wu
Dawang's discretion, his willingness to accept humiliation in order to protect a woman's reputation,
was of course very much to his credit as a soldier,
and as a man of honour. But lurking deep within
this generous nobility of spirit, could there also have
been a tiny, selfish desire to savour this delicious
secret alone? Since the curtain had only just gone

up on this grand romantic drama, did he perhaps feel it would be wrong to spoil the plot for his audience before the performance had properly begun? Remembering, as his Instructor droned on, how the Division Commander had trampled on that ill-fated head, Wu Dawang placed his foot on a sturdy clump of grass. While the Political Instructor was interrogating him as to what, precisely, he had done to offend Liu Lian, he twisted his foot from side to side, as one would stub out a cigarette, imagining he was grinding her face into the ground: her mouth, her red lips and white teeth, her forehead and her high, straight nose. As the Political Instructor warmed to his theme, Wu Dawang moved on down her body until, at the thought of her marvellous breasts, his belligerent foot faltered and shrank from the impressive hollow it had made — defeated by a bosom.

The moon had now reached the southwest. Unnoticed by Wu Dawang, the drinkers had dispersed back to their respective companies and the barracks were quiet. The breeze was still lapping about, rustling across the drill ground. He examined the hole he'd made, its edges scattered with displaced yellow-brown earth and crushed plant stalks. The strong, sharp smell of raw soil flavoured the cool night air. Guiltily contemplating, by the light of the moon, the mess he had made, he nudged the loose soil back with his boot.

'Go to bed,' the Political Instructor repeated, 'it's getting late. But remember what I said: you won't get a third chance. If the Division Commander's wife has really taken against you, you're done for.'

'Thank you, Sir,' Wu Dawang finally responded. 'If I wasn't in uniform, I'd kneel down and kowtow to you right here.'

'What kind of talk is that for a revolutionary,' the Political Instructor chided him, giving him a light clip around the ear before heading back to his dormitory.

Wu Dawang followed on behind; back to bed.

AS ANY GOOD READER OF fiction will know, the progress of a story is dependent not only on the personalities of its main characters, but also on the experiences that have brought them to where they are today—to their narrative present. And it was now that Wu Dawang's own personal history exerted a truly decisive influence. One light flutter of the butterfly's wings sent the globe of fate spinning in an entirely new direction.

As Wu Dawang lay sleeplessly on his bed, reflecting on the twists and turns his life had taken, he eventually fixed on the question of his marriage. Six years ago, at the ripe old age of twenty-two, he had been a simple farmer in Wujiagou, a village nestling among the mountains of Funiu in western Henan. Every day, he would start work when the sun rose and stop when it sank. Just as a weed starved of sunlight or a wild sapling deprived of rain struggles for survival, he lived in ignorance of the most basic and instinctive of life's comforts and pleasures. His father had been taken ill and died years ago, leaving a widow and her only son to eke out a miserable existence in the poor, remote, drought-stricken mountain village they called home.

Luckily for Wu Dawang, however, his mother insisted—at great personal cost—on keeping him in school until he was sixteen.

Thanks to these years of education, he became the accountant for Wujiagou's production team—the collective farming unit into which the Communist government had organized the village.

Time passed, and he reached marriageable age. More time passed, but still no match could be found for him. Just as he was on the verge of despair at his marital prospects, it so happened that the leader of the village production team fell ill before a rush harvest meeting at the local commune, and appointed Wu Dawang as his deputy. At the meeting, the commune accountant, one Zhao, needed someone to help him copy out a list of attendees' names so that he could issue each with expenses (three steamed buns and one *yuan*).

So Wu Dawang volunteered.

This chance assignment would change the course of Wu Dawang's drab existence. For, unbeknownst to Wu, although the accountant's wife and children were still classified as peasants and therefore drew their income from the land, Zhao himself was on the state payroll. He therefore qualified as a government official—as a Someone on a social and professional footing with the director of the commune himself.

Zhao was in his midforties and of medium height, with eyebrows drawn so faintly across his broad face they were hardly worth having. When Wu Dawang delivered the list to him, he was sitting in an easy chair behind his desk. He glanced over the document, then looked up at the young man. 'What village are you from?'

'Wujiagou.'

'You're very young to be a team leader, aren't you?'

'I'm the accountant, I'm only standing in because the team leader's ill.'

'An accountant, you say? How old are you?'

'Twenty-two.'

'How far did you get in school?'

'Junior middle school.'

'Engaged?'

'Not yet.'

Perhaps because Zhao, as an accountant, had a soft spot for his fellow professionals, or perhaps because he had a bureaucrat's eye for talent, the interview went Wu Dawang's way from there on in. After several glances up at Wu, then back at his list of names, Zhao broke into a smile. 'Nice handwriting,' he complimented him, 'and in ballpoint, too. Quite the master calligrapher.'

And so it was that the regularity of Wu Dawang's writing hand transformed his personal prospects. One day, long after the rush harvest and planting had come and gone, when the new corn seedlings were already an inch high, the team leader came back from a trip to market with news for Wu Dawang. 'The commune accountant Zhao has taken a shine to you,' he reported, in great excitement. 'He's asked me to bring you to see him.'

Wu Dawang accompanied his leader the dozen or so miles to Zhao Village, uncharacteristically well turned out in a new blue jacket and pair of black twill trousers. Although both were borrowed, this getup was close enough to a military uniform to give him an unmistakable dash—and, most importantly, to convince Zhao that here was the very fellow for his only daughter.

It was in his unusually spacious and well-apportioned three-roomed tiled house that the accountant revealed Wu Dawang's new career direction to him. 'Before the year's out, Dawang, I'll fix it for you to join the army.'

A career in the military, Zhao said, was not just about education and training. It was also a way into the Party, to commendations; it was the ladder to promotion, to becoming an official. 'And once you're an official, you can get an urban registration permit for my daughter—Ezi here—so she can come and live the good life in the city with you.' This was every peasant's dream: to leave the uncertain, never-ending toil of farming for the comforts of the city and a state-allocated job.

Wu Dawang progressed amenably through the initial stages of his future father-in-law's plan. Toward the end of the year he left to join the army, and the second major phase of his life began. On the training grounds of the People's Liberation Army, his simple virtues of honesty, industry and patience served him admirably, helping him to negotiate the challenges of the military life. To him, the hard physical exercise dreaded by so many of his comrades was no more punishing than the busy seasons of the farming year. Political study classes—a source of spiritual torture to some—he found no more tedious than the weeks of slack that followed planting or harvesting. Wu Dawang read his newspapers, studied editorials and perused documents in the safe knowledge that at the next meal there would be as many steamed rolls as he could eat, as well as meat. As he wore clothes, slept under quilts and ate food supplied, free of charge, by the government, every day in the army felt like New Year in the village he had just left. With a daily life of such luxury and ease, getting up earlier than everyone else to sweep the floor, or staying up later than everyone else to read editorials and note down in his diary all he had learnt and thought for perusal by his superiors, practicing drill on Sundays, washing trousers and socks for his comrades-in-arms—all this seemed no hardship at all.

In public, Wu Dawang was careful to ensure his actions spoke louder than his words, and that his

capacity for work was matched only by his willingness to embrace criticism. To think hard but say
little, to channel ingenuity into practical ends and
to blunt intelligence into worthy dullness—these
were the survival strategies that Wu Dawang picked
up from the veterans around him. Although Wu
Dawang had not yet learnt from personal experience
that advancing with caution permits a safe retreat,
he none the less stuck firmly to this principle in his
new life.

After only a year in the army, however, the sky
fell in on Wu Dawang's world. His mother was
struck down by cirrhosis of the liver and, all too soon,
summoned her son back to Wujiagou to attend her
deathbed. 'If you want to do your duty by me before I die,' the old lady said to him, taking him by
the hand, 'then get yourself married, here in the village, so I know I'll have a daughter-in-law to tend
my grave.'

So Wu Dawang went to see his prospective father-
in-law, who chewed his request over thoughtfully.
'Have you won any commendations yet?' he eventually asked.

'No, not yet.'

'Have they let you join the Party?'

'Not yet.'

'Are you likely to get promoted?'

'Hard to say.'

After further meditation, Zhao heaved a long sigh. 'Don't think me heartless,' he said. 'It's just that people have high hopes. It's natural; everyone wants the best for their daughters. You're not in the Party, you've no commendations, no prospect of getting promoted. What kind of life can you offer my little girl?'

Wu Dawang collapsed to his knees, the tears streaming down his face. 'Father,' he begged, 'let me call you Father. If I don't achieve everything you ask, if I fail to win commendations, join the Party, become an official and move Ezi to the city, if I don't find her a good job and give her a good life, I'll never show my face around here again, not even for my funeral.'

Zhao sank back into deep thought. 'You really think you can manage all that?' he asked at length.

'I'll put it in writing.' And so, on a blank piece of paper, he inscribed the following pledge:

After I, Wu Dawang, marry Ezi, I solemnly promise to do everything within my power to ensure I earn commendations within one year, join the Party within two and become an official within three. If I fail and am consequently unable to move the aforesaid Zhao Ezi to a new home in the city where she can eat steamed rolls every day, I, Wu Dawang, will never show my face, dead or alive, in Wujiagou again. If Ezi permits me to return, I swear to serve her in any way she chooses for the rest of my life. If I utter a single word of complaint I deserve to die in agony.

Almost as soon as the ink was dry on this prenuptial agreement, Wu Dawang was married. Two weeks later, his mother departed this world with a smile on her face. And from this point on, Wu Dawang was no longer master of his own destiny or of his marital happiness.

When he returned to the army, he toiled. But others also toiled, and he did not earn a commendation.

The following year, he struggled. But others also struggled, and he was not admitted into the Party.

As he laboured, to no avail, through those two long years, every time a letter arrived from his wife or father-in-law, asking how he was getting on, his panic mounted. A form of despair took hold of him. Every year, when his name failed yet again to make the list of new Party members and commendations, he would even contemplate suicide. But, just as desperation truly set in, the post of Sergeant of the Catering Squad fell vacant. It was well known that, although the work itself was filthy and exhausting, Catering Squad soldiers advanced quickly through the ranks — precisely because of the uncongenial nature of their duties. As a result, eight soldiers from across the three platoons and nine squads of the company vied to fill this single position — every single one of them, like Wu Dawang, of ambitious peasant origin.

The company's Captain was away on officer training at the time and the Political Instructor was lording it over the company like a little emperor. One word from him, and the prize would be yours. When the Instructor's wife came for a visit, the eight hopefuls were forever haring over to his room to sweep his floor or wash his wife's clothes, until his head was fairly turned with indecision. One weekend, as he continued to wrestle with the dilemma, the Political Instructor returned to find his own son riding on Wu Dawang's back, slapping his head as if he was cracking a whip against a horse's neck. 'Faster! Faster!'

he yelped, as Wu Dawang cavorted around the room on all fours, even letting out the odd whinny for added effect.

Outraged, the Political Instructor yanked his son off Wu Dawang's back, cuffed his offspring around the head, then turned to roar at his subordinate. 'Where's your self-respect, man, crawling about on the floor like that?'

'I've always loved serving others,' Wu Dawang explained, standing up and brushing the earth off his hands and knees. 'It's how I put the theory of Serve the People into practice.'

The Political Instructor stared at him, failing to conceal his amazement. 'Is that what you think Serve the People means?' he asked after a pause, an edge of uncertainty in his voice.

'If a person won't Serve the People in practice,' he replied, 'how can he Serve the People in theory?'

For the next two weeks, the eight candidates kept up their extra-hours campaign of sweeping and mopping the Political Instructor's floor, of trimming and peeling vegetables for him, of buying sweets for his son and pounds of dates and walnuts for his wife. Over and above all this, however, Wu Dawang did something none of his competitors did: he made a habit of taking the instructor's son out to play, galloping around on all fours if the boy wanted to ride on his back, howling up at the heavens if he wanted to hear a dog bark. The smile never left the boy's face—until bedtime when he'd cry out in his sleep for his beloved uncle Wu Dawang.

Finally, the Political Instructor called Wu Dawang in for a momentous interview.

'What,' he asked, 'is the first, and only principle of Serving the People?'

'To serve others as you would wish to be served yourself,' Wu Dawang replied.

'How do we give our lives meaning?'

'By bringing glory to the enterprise of Serving the People every day of our lives and by devoting ourselves as absolutely to serving the needy as a son should devote himself to serving his parents.'

'Good,' the Political Instructor nodded, 'well put. Simple, but thoughtful; practical, but idealistic; an accomplished marriage of theory and practice. My only quibble would be with the parent–son analogy.'

Wu Dawang was thus formally transferred to the Catering Squad as Deputy Sergeant, taking over responsibility for the company's food and water. From this point on, his career prospects were transformed. In the next year and a half, before he was appointed to the household of the Division Commander himself, Wu Dawang not only jumped a rank to full Sergeant, but was also admitted to the Party. With the help of his Political Instructor, commendations and awards became commonplace. Only one clause of his prenuptial agreement remained unfulfilled: promotion to officialdom. First his blood pressure tested too high, then other companies won the promotion quotas; another time, a soldier in another battalion beat him to it, then the *yin* fell out with the *yang*. For whatever reason, the four-pocket jacket that distinguished officials from the hoi polloi remained tantalizingly out of reach.

There could be little doubt that Wu Dawang's transfer to the Division Commander's house more than doubled his chances of promotion but, just as he had begun to hope the prize was within reach, Liu Lian suddenly brought his coolly untroubled emotional depths to a turbulent boil. It was like offering a former smoker an opium pipe, threatening to hurl him from absolute privation into an abyss of excess.

Even though Wu Dawang could see that the bottom of this particular abyss was cushioned with a dense, perfumed carpet of flowers, he feared the lack of restraint with which he was likely to respond, should he permit himself to sink into it.

The opium analogy might help us to understand Wu Dawang's particular response toward the naked Liu Lian—his overwrought hesitation in the face of this delectable feast. Once he had stepped back from temptation, some sense of regret was almost inevitable. So far, he had paid for it in the currency of almost a whole night's sleep. After hours of restless reflection, lying still fully clothed in bed, he concluded that resistance would be useless and, most likely, counterproductive.

To contemporary eyes, life back then must seem lacking in emotional depth. More often than not, however, psychological complexity exists only in novels, as authors fill in details absent from protagonists' actual thoughts. As emotion, like comedy, is essentially immediate, its outward expressions tend to the superficial rather than the profound. That night, as the sky began to lighten, Wu Dawang finally dozed off and dreamed he was in carnal embrace with Liu Lian. On waking, he discovered a sticky smear across the underside of his quilt. Mortified, he pinched his own thigh into purple bruises of self-loathing. Then, from under his pillow, he took out a letter from his wife that had arrived three days ago and, while the dormitory was still asleep, reread it under his quilt by the light of his torch. It contained little by way of news, only that the wheat was now in and the autumn crops sown. She'd cut her hand harvesting the wheat and it had bled a lot but was better now. Because she'd had no one to look after their son while she was working, she'd left him tied up with rope in the shade of a tree at the top of the field with a few locusts and pieces of tile to play with. While her back was turned, he'd put a locust in his mouth and nearly choked on it. His eyes had almost popped out of their sockets, the letter said.

Wu Dawang wept as he pictured his son so close to death. He folded up the letter, got out of bed, left his slumbering company to its dreams, and strode with new resolution off to the Division Commander's house. A night's contemplation and a re-reading of his letter had set a new plan in motion. His behaviour, in the next phase of our story, was set to switch from the passive to the active, as he strove to master the situation he found himself in; to appoint himself the chief protagonist of the narrative, the great helmsman steering the course of this particular love affair. But this was no high-flown struggle for clear moral victory—just one individual finding the courage to challenge his destiny.

For the record, he did not consider that matters were beyond repair. All that had happened was that Liu Lian had informed his immediate superiors that she no longer wanted him as her cook. He could resolve the situation himself, he thought; he could win her over. Hatred for Liu Lian, and for himself, welled up inside. He was the one who had wrecked a perfectly workable status quo, and so he would have to be the one to make amends—as if, after flouting some basic rule of dining etiquette, he now had to down a cup of spirits as a forfeit. He would do whatever was necessary. And in any case, the actual forfeit in store was hardly a humiliation or punishment, but rather held out the promise of romance and promotion.

At this point in our story, the depths that his relationship with Liu Lian would later reach lay hidden in the shallows of his pragmatic calculations. In fact, in the majority of cases, emotional complications are no such thing. Pull a knotty problem apart and, as likely as not, you will find at its heart an equation of overwhelming simplicity. Wu Dawang's return to the Division Commander's house—a decision dictated by professional ambition and marital obligation—can be explained in terms just as straightforward.

As he left his company, the horizon to the east was beginning to glimmer orange and a milky brightness was spreading in the sky directly over the barracks. Heading toward the Division Commander's house through the dawn light, as he had done almost every day for the past six months, he encountered his company's Captain, on his way back after a patrol check. Though his eyes were still blurry with sleep, the Captain's mind was clearly operational.

'Off to work then?' he asked, stopping right in Wu Dawang's path.

Wu Dawang mumbled an affirmative as he saluted and bid his Captain good morning.

After returning the salute, the Captain turned to carry on his way, then stopped, as if he had suddenly thought of something. 'Wu Dawang,' he asked, 'what must you remember, above all else, when working for a senior officer?'

'Don't say what I shouldn't say, and don't do what I shouldn't do.'

'Wrong.'

'To serve the Division Commander and his family,' he corrected himself, 'is to Serve the People.'

'Better. Now say it again, but shout it this time.'

After glancing around at the dormitories behind him, he repeated the sacred principle louder, but still way below full volume. 'To Serve the Division Commander and His Family is to Serve the People.'

'I said shout!' the Captain bellowed, glaring at Wu Dawang.

'They're all asleep.' He glanced back, a frustrated zeal flickering across his face.

'If I tell you to shout, that's an order. There's an extra commendation in it for you if you manage to wake them up.' Then, as if drilling a new recruit, he retreated half a pace, tilted his head back and shouted, 'One—two—three—'

And, just as if he were an eager new recruit, Wu Dawang roared out, with the relentlessly forceful rhythm of the drill ground: 'To Serve the Division Commander and His Family is to Serve the People!' He looked at the Captain, who beamed with pleasure.

'That'll do. Off you go now.'

Wu Dawang watched the Captain disappear into the barracks, before at last carrying on his way. Behind him, the soldiers he had startled awake were peering out through windows and doorways. Their looking done, they soon returned to their beds, as if all were right as could be with the world.

MOST OF THE SENIOR OFFICERS were already up and awake, each exercising in their private court-yards and waiting for reveille to sound and summon them to supervise the morning's drills. Entering the main compound, Wu Dawang exchanged nods and greetings with the sentry. After saluting the Deputy Division Commander, he took a key out of his pocket and opened the small iron gate that would let him into Number One. Latching it behind him, he turned back toward the house, intending to go around to the kitchen and start preparing Liu Lian's favourite breakfast of lotus seed rice soup.

Imagine his surprise, however, when he discov-ered that Liu Lian—whom he had never seen out of bed before end-of-drill had sounded—had chosen to rise today before reveille and had seated herself in the yard in front of the house, wearing the army uniform that had spent the past five years folded up in a cupboard. Wu Dawang had never once seen her in it. The stiff scarlet insignia on her collar threw her pallor into even greater relief. She looked as if she'd slept as badly as her orderly. On both men and women, army uniforms came up baggy, ill-fitting, and somehow had a levelling effect: they made the young look older and the old younger; the attractive plainer and the plain more attractive. There she sat in front of the house, her bleary-eyed face sagging with fatigue, as if she had just completed Mao's Long March of 10,000 miles, fighting the Nationalist enemy all the way.

Disconcerted both by her presence in the yard and by her mode of dress, Wu Dawang fixed a smile across his face. 'How come you're up so early, Aunt?'

His arrival had clearly taken her just as much by surprise. She glanced at him a couple of times before answering his question, in a tone somewhere between chilly and freezing, with another question. 'Didn't your Political Instructor speak to you?'

He lowered his eyes. 'Yes, he did, but I want you to give me another chance. If I fail to give satisfaction again today, I'll take myself straight back to barracks.'

He looked up at her stony face. That one night seemed to have spun a web of fine wrinkles out from the corners of her eyes. She was beginning to look her thirty-two years. A woman in her early thirties, of course, was still young enough to be his sister, to set hearts racing, to possess a ripe allure. But Liu Lian didn't normally look her age; it must have been the uniform playing tricks on her. Or her lack of sleep: perhaps she'd been sitting there all night, staring expressionlessly out across the courtyard. More than anything, he wanted to tell her she looked tired, that she should go back to her room and rest, but his courage failed him. Now that he had rejected yesterday's overture, an absolute darkness reigned between them. He gazed timidly at her, head slightly bowed as if awaiting judgement, which, after subjecting him to a long, steady stare, she eventually pronounced.

'Don't bother with my soup this morning,' she instructed dully, getting up from her chair. 'Just boil me a couple of eggs, then go back to barracks.' Without waiting a second longer for him to ask her anything else, she returned upstairs, alone. Her footsteps, the slam of the door behind her, pounded on his eardrums.

Things were turning out worse than Wu Dawang had expected. The reveille blared over the tannoy, plunging the barracks into fresh fits of over-enthusiasm. Wu Dawang reminded himself that he'd been in the army five long years, that he had impeccable experience of Serving the People, that he was a paragon of political correctness, the pride of his company, a model Party member. He now recast his already deep understanding of 'Serve the People' into a weapon for overcoming his present difficulties and the destiny they pointed to. After Liu Lian's footsteps had died away, he moved swiftly to the kitchen. There he set a pot of water to boil, broke two eggs into a bowl, whisked them together, added two spoonfuls of white sugar, then trickled the simmering water into the sweetened viscous mixture, beating and turning it with chopsticks as he did so. In much less than a minute, he had ready a piping hot bowl of golden egg-drop soup. While waiting for it to cool a little, fresh inspiration came to him. Taking up a pen and paper, he leaned over the kitchen table and quickly composed a searching statement of self-criticism, acknowledging the serious errors in his understanding of 'Serve the People'. He then carried both soup and self-criticism upstairs.

Standing at the door to her room, he knocked lightly a couple of times. 'Sister,' he mustered the courage to call out, 'your egg soup's ready, I've brought it up to you.'

A listless response drawled out from inside: 'Leave it on the dining table and go back to barracks. Ask your superiors to send the new orderly over as soon as they can.'

While not quite what he'd hoped, this reply nevertheless was largely in keeping with the tone of their most recent exchanges.

Only briefly put off, he tried again. 'I understand if you want me out of the house, but your soup's getting cold. Will you let me bring it in to you one last time?' Taking liberal advantage of her silence, he pushed open the door. She was sitting on the edge of the bed, having changed out of her uniform and into a pink polyester blouse with a neat collar and pale blue, straight-legged trousers of the style fashionable at the time. Suddenly, she looked exuberantly youthful again, though the sour, aggrieved expression her face had worn outside seemed to have taken deeper hold of her features.

Setting the egg soup down on the table, he glanced nervously at her. 'It's getting cold,' he repeated, 'better eat it quick.' He held his confessional out to her: 'I wrote a self-criticism. I'll write another if you don't think this one goes far enough.'

She glared at him, ignoring the scrap of paper in his hand. 'So you realize you made a mistake?'

'I know. Let me put it right.'

'It's too late now. I want you to go back to your company. I've told your Political Instructor to have you discharged at the end of the year, so you can go home to look after your wife.'

Although this communiqué was delivered at normal, conversational volume, its meaning exploded in Wu Dawang's head, inducing a numbing dizziness. He'd thought his voluntary self-criticism would melt away all the tension between them beautifully, just as the sun rising in the east thaws a river's dawn veneer of ice. But there she sat, impervious to his efforts at reconciliation. The scene at dusk the day before began to come back to him. He remembered how she'd lain on the bed, naked, waiting for him to take off his clothes and join her there. This was no sudden rush of blood to the head, no act of blind desperation brought on by the Division Commander's absence; it was a brave and long premeditated step into uncharted territory. His cowardice had first wounded her to the core, then planted a deep seed of contempt for him.

Now—now Wu Dawang began to rue what, only yesterday, had struck him as a response of perfect rectitude. It wasn't his forfeiting of the opportunity to sleep with Liu Lian that he was regretting, but rather the cataclysmic consequences that this rejection now seemed to threaten. It is practically impossible to evoke here the genuine terror Wu Dawang felt at the prospect of his glorious future plunging back into darkness—as if at the flick of a switch. He looked up at Liu Lian, his self-criticism trembling at the end of his outstretched arm. The end-of-drill bell briefly drowned the room in sound, then died away. The bleak quiet returned, pressing suffocatingly down on him, as if a tower, or a stretch of the Great Wall or a mountain range were weighing upon his skull.

As tears started in his eyes, he fell to his knees before Liu Lian, who seemed as surprised by his sudden obeisance as he was himself. He knew that he needed to say something else, but couldn't think what it should be. Until, finally, his agitation forced a sobbed entreaty out of him.

'Give me another chance,' he begged. 'If I don't Serve the People this time round, I'll go straight out and throw myself under a bus, or in front of target practice. Either way, you'll never hear from me again.'

Perhaps it was the subtle hint in this outburst that at last moved Liu Lian. Or perhaps it was the sight of him kneeling before her that thawed her icy heart. Although she didn't tell him to get up, she shifted her position slightly on the bed. 'And how, exactly, do you propose to Serve the People?' she asked.

'However you want me to.'

'Run naked three times around the drill ground.'

He looked up at her, unsure whether she was playing with him, or seriously testing the sincerity of his pledge. Putting his self-criticism down on the floor in front of him, he placed his hand on his breast. There he knelt, as if in combat readiness, as if—like an arrow drawn across a bow string—waiting for the word to begin his naked sprint.

As things stood, matters had now swung from the deadly serious to the unimaginably ridiculous—to a level of absurdity beyond Wu Dawang's own comprehension, but still artistically consistent with the fantastical parameters of our story. Neither character, in fact, had grasped the full ludicrousness of the scene they were acting out, or of their roles within it. Perhaps, in very particular circumstances, emotional truth can shine only through the curtain of farce, while earnest restraint will always fail to ring true. Maybe absurdity is the state that all affairs of the heart are, finally, destined for: the ultimate and only test of worth.

His hand travelled up to his collar.

'Serve the People,' she said. 'Take it off.'

Off came his jacket, the buttons popping one by one, revealing an undershirt emblazoned with the message 'Serve the People'.

'Serve the People,' she said. 'Take it off.'

Off came the shirt.

'On you go. Serve the People.'

After a moment's hesitation, he tugged off his trousers, unveiling his athletically muscular form, just as she had exposed herself to him the evening before.

Their gazes locked, crackling with antagonistic passion. A lustful light flickered in their eyes—a tongue
of flame about to lick a pile of dry tinder alight. And
as their desire smouldered through the thinning air
of the room, Liu Lian found the exact, the only words
that the moment required. 'Serve the People—go on,
serve them, serve them, serve them . . .'

VI

OUR STORY HAS SO FAR followed a course that most readers will have anticipated. And once the curtain was properly lifted on this affair, the performance took on its own, largely foreseeable momentum, even while its finale remained uncertain. As he acted out the part allotted to him, however, Wu Dawang's thoughts would often stray involuntarily back to his passionless past, initially thwarting him in his impulse to wallow, uninhibited, in the mire of sexual bliss.

It remained a matter of some mystery to him how, precisely, his married life had become so claustrophobically joyless. Like a melon plant that produced only shrivelled seeds, his advances towards Ezi never achieved their desired logical result—real intimacy and warmth.

Until they found themselves alone together, their wedding night had progressed conventionally enough.

The ceremony had been conducted and the party broken up, after a respectable interval, by the village team leader. Once the children appointed to haze the nuptial chamber had been chased away into the evening dark and the room had at last fallen quiet, his hands had fumbled for his wife's body, the excitement of the celebration still upon them.

She looked him straight in the eye. 'Are you a good soldier?' she asked.

'All my officers tell me I am,' he replied.

'Why are you manhandling me like this then? Aren't you ashamed of yourself?'

With these words, Wu Dawang realized that a certain something—a thing called love that you read about in books—would be missing from their union. He sat on their nuptial bed, gazing across at his wife, feeling the bleakness radiate out from the heart of their marriage, from their garish, red-lacquered bed. It was a vague, sorrowful regret for an absent love, made all the more poignant by her own failure to sense it.

He dressed and walked to the door.

'Where are you going?' she asked. 'It's the middle of the night.'

'Go to sleep. I'm going to the toilet.'

Afterward, he sat alone in the courtyard, sunk in desolation. When he stared up at the pale crescent moon floating amid the clouds, he felt a vertiginous tremor of fear — a fear that it might fall from the sky.

The April stars sprinkled their light over the courtyard in the middle of his family's thatched, three-room, mud-brick compound. Sitting in its centre, serenaded by cicadas and smelling the spring grass on the air, he gazed blankly up at the silver moon, as if communing with it on the subject of his marriage.

In the end, of the two newlyweds it was Wu Dawang who broke first, who could stand the torment of sexual deprivation no longer. Eventually, when the moon sank and the stars faded, he went back inside, undressed silently and lay down beside her, the scent of the paste used to festoon the walls with proclamations of 'Double Happiness' still hanging faintly over the room. Though she was in bed, Ezi was not asleep and from under her quilt wafted the earthy, headily unfamiliar smell of a peasant girl. 'It's almost light,' she murmured, 'where have you been?' When he pulled back the quilt, sultry with her body warmth, he suddenly encountered her innocently rustic scent. The room was dark apart from the pale dawn haze at the window. He allowed himself two quiet, cautious inhalations, two lungs full of night air infused with that feminine fragrance. He tried to slip under the covers, to suppress all desire for her by the strength of his will, through the military self-discipline that he had learnt over the past year. Yet in that bed, under that quilt, his hand found itself moving recklessly down over her shoulder. In the moment it took him to compare the feel of her skin with silk, his willpower was broken and he was upon her.

Although she too was clearly ablaze, prey to exactly the same primitive, instinctive desire, she struggled out from underneath him, shrank backward—as if flinching from a needle—and pushed his hands from her. Once more, they lay side by side in the still night, at an impasse.

'You're my wife now, Zhao Ezi,' he said. 'If you stop me one more time, I'll have to force you.'

'You can have me,' she answered, 'but I want you to promise me three things first.'

'And they are?'

'One, next year when you come home on leave, I want you to bring me an army uniform.'

'Fine, I promise.'

'Two, I want you to earn a commendation every year, and to telegram me the good news as soon as you get it. It's not just about the honour, the production team will award me ten *yuan*, too.'

'Agreed. And the third?'

'I want you to kneel in front of me, right now, on the bed, and swear you'll work hard after you go back to the army, obey your commanders and do whatever it takes to become a Party official so I can move to the city.'

'I already promised all that in the pledge I wrote for your father.'

'I don't care. I want you to swear it all over again, kneeling in front of me. Then you can have me.'

He knelt on the bed, facing his wife. 'If I, Wu Dawang, fail to work hard and obey the Party, I deserve to be struck five times by lightning. If in this lifetime I fail to win promotion and give you, Zhao Ezi, a home in the city, may Heaven above condemn me to die without descendants.'

Whether out of hunger for professional advancement, or yearning for his wife's curvaceous form, Wu Dawang delivered his oath in low fervent tones, with the solemn, almost devout urgency born of intense impatience. His declaration made, he studied her face. 'Will that do?' he asked softly.

'I believe you.'

Then, in one decisive manoeuvre, he drew the body of his new wife—the body that had been his from the start of their negotiations but which she had nevertheless resolved to barter against some better, future existence—to him.

With this, sexual intimacy began between them—but love ended.

From that point on, he was allowed to have his way with her every night. But, as regular as clockwork, just as he reached orgasm she would pipe up with: 'You must work hard when you return to the army, Dawang.' In another, more mundane context, these words would have struck him as no more than an affectionate reminder, but spoken on the brink of climax they chilled him like a drenching in icy water. The vague semblance of affection that existed between them thus became as fragile as a sheet of sodden paper, useless as a medium for expressing emotional truths.

FOR WU DAWANG, IT WAS the contrast with his dispiritingly frigid marriage that truly validated his affair with Liu Lian, that gave him eyes to appreciate, once he had stepped under her mosquito net, the glories of love. To his mind, the frequency with which he and Liu Lian made love represented the soundest, the most sublime proof of their feelings for each other. For close on two months, day and night they luxuriated in passion's lake, dazzled by its surface shimmer, intoxicated by each glittering droplet. Regrettably perhaps, neither understood that a dangerously raw sexual undercurrent was choosing its moment to tug them both down.

Not long after their liaison began, Liu Lian had telephoned the Captain and Political Instructor of Wu Dawang's company to say that she was afraid of being alone in the house at night with the Division Commander away. Having taken her criticism to heart, she told them, Wu Dawang had given complete satisfaction ever since. As a result, for the rest of her husband's stay in Beijing she would prefer it if Sergeant Wu slept in the house rather than returning to barracks every evening.

Wu Dawang's immediate superiors readily agreed, emphasizing to Liu Lian that any inadequacy on the part of her orderly reflected directly on the company itself. If she found him guilty of further oversights or carelessness, she should address her criticism to him, then lodge an extra complaint against them and the company's Party representatives. And that is how easily the scene was set for this extraordinary affair. So easily, in fact, that in time its hero and heroine came to forget that it was only theatre, and not life itself. Like method actors, they played their roles for real.

Every day Wu Dawang still tended the vegetable garden at the back of the house, and the flowers and shrubs at the front. But what had been a professional duty now became a performance given for the benefit of passersby, to reassure them, as they glanced in through the gate, that all was exactly as it ever had been: that Liu Lian was still the Division

Commander's wife, and Wu Dawang the Division Commander's General Orderly. Only our chief protagonists could know of the great, underlying change that had taken place behind this façade.

Before, he'd always needed to watch the time as he worked in the garden, returning to the kitchen to have meals ready exactly on time. Now, however, he dawdled outside as he pleased. When mealtimes approached, Liu Lian would beckon him in from the doorway—not to cook for her, but to keep her company while she cooked; another symptom of the revolutionary goings-on inside Compound Number One. The first meal she'd ever cooked him was breakfast, which she brought to his bedside just as he'd brought her the bowl of egg-drop soup that first, fateful morning. Waking from the deep slumber that follows a night of passion, he'd found the sun streaming in through the curtains and Liu Lian gone. Pulling himself up with a start, he found her sitting next to him on the edge of the bed, gazing at him as he slept.

'Heavens,' he began to apologize, 'I haven't got your breakfast ready.' She stroked his cheek, her face breaking into a sweet smile, as if his return to consciousness had instantly driven away melancholy.

'It's my turn to Serve the People,' she said. Lifting up the bowl of egg soup she had prepared, she fed it to him, mouthful by mouthful. She took the last few drops into her own mouth, then gently released them into his, with a touch of her lips. In thanks for this bowl of soup and for the gift of a love whose depths he'd not yet fathomed, he then slowly undressed her until she stood—like a jade pillar—naked before the bed. Although they'd lived for days as husband and wife, although they'd made love more times than he could remember, this was the first time he'd admired, with such lingering calm, the whole of her—her marvellous, nude form, illuminated by the single, oblique strip of sunlight that a crack in the curtains had let in. He considered her hair, her pink and white complexion, her body, as flawlessly fair as the moon and stars and unblemished by a single mole or imperfection, her breasts, still as gravity-defying as a twenty-year-old's. Her stomach had not a single line across it, not a whisper of a crease or mark or blotch. A hand skimming over the silky skin under her breasts—as white as if it'd been dusted with crushed Osmanthus petals— might have imagined it was touching a moonbeam.

There she stood, in that shaft of sunlight, her face communicating a slight bashfulness, permitting his caresses as though she were a living statue tolerating the final refinements of her sculptor. Her hands, which she'd been running through his hair, weakened, and then her legs. A feeling of light-headedness was spreading through her body, quickening the tremble that had taken hold of her limbs. And yet his hands and eyes continued their work, moving slowly down from her breasts. Tears of ecstasy clung to the tips of her lower eyelashes, and swayed as if about to fall, until she burst into urgent sobs.

'What's wrong?' he asked.

'I feel terribly dizzy,' she replied.

'You'd better get dressed,' he said, alarmed. 'I'll phone the Division hospital.'

'No, there's no need for that. Just carry me to the bed and go on kissing me, touching me wherever you want. Forget I'm the Division Commander's wife — for the time being I'm your wife and you can have free run of me.'

He lifted her weak, limp form onto the bed, as one would put a baby down to sleep, then began kissing her with a crazed intensity, every tiny part of her, from her hair, forehead and nose downward—now delicately, like a dragonfly skimming the surface of a lake, now insistently, forgetting everything but a feverish desire to consume her with his lips. If he lingered too long on a particular spot, her hands would eventually caress his head with a gentle reminder, prompting a reluctant, regretful farewell as he continued on his way. When his lips explored her own, the tears streamed—with a kind of joyful sorrow—from her eyes to pool in dark circles on the green sheet and thick red velvet pillow. When, however, his tongue at last insinuated its way between her legs, her hands fell—as lifelessly as two pieces of rope—from his head onto the bed, and her cries died away into an abrupt silence.

He immediately stopped everything he was doing.

He looked up to discover she'd taken on a deathly, waxen pallor.

She had, he could see, fainted—from excitement.

The room had fallen as quiet as the grave. He circled around and around her, shaking her, calling out to her, his sweat dripping onto her naked body and the rumpled bed. A few seconds later, however, he came round from his panic and recovered some sense of calm. Recalling his basic first aid training, he pulled on his underpants, opened the window and door, laid a towel out in the doorway, picked Liu Lian up and placed her down on it. And there she lay, peacefully, like a large white fish.

The breeze blew in through the window, bringing a welcome coolness. A large cloud had passed in front of the sun, shading the Division Commander's compound like a parasol. As Liu Lian maintained her silent prostration, Wu Dawang kept an equally silent watch over her. A few times he considered pinching her, or giving her mouth-to-mouth resuscitation, but always chose to stay where he was instead: unmoving, by her side. Gloomy thoughts of home forced their way into his mind: of his wife Zhao Ezi writing about the harvest, about tying their son to that tree, about the child almost choking to death on a locust. These thoughts triggered in him a peasant's violent, covetous hatred of the easy, sophisticated city life and its glorious free love that could never be his. He stared at Liu Lian, a dreadful hope taking hold of him. How marvellous it would be, he thought, if she really did die. The moment he'd thought it, this idea somehow took root in his head and grew into a powerful impulse to place his hands on that long, smooth, slender white neck of hers.

Fortunately, at that very moment, she woke up.

Tilting her head to one side, she took in her surroundings, including Wu Dawang. She then pulled herself weakly up into a sitting position. 'It's been worth it,' she said, 'it's all been worth it. I can die happy now.'

He shivered to hear her talk of dying, as if she had seen right through him, and into the terrible, ridiculous idea that had just seized him. Nervous that his murderous instincts had in some way betrayed themselves, he leaned over attentively and took her hand. 'How do you feel?' he asked her. 'You scared me half to death. You fainted, it was all my fault.'

She looked gratefully at him, tears wetting the corners of her eyes, and stroked his face. 'Would you bring me my clothes?' she asked. He picked them up from the table and helped her get dressed, the two of them still sitting on the towel, talking away, holding each other's hands.

'I wish you were my husband,' she said.

'You're the Division Commander's wife,' he reminded her. 'You're the envy of every woman in China.'

'That may be.' After a brief, slanting glance away, she looked straight back at him. A blush returned to her cheeks. 'Do you know why the Commander's first wife divorced him?'

He answered her only with an expression of surprise.

'He's impotent.'

He continued to stare at her in silent, mounting amazement.

But she had nothing more to say. After heaving a long, pained sigh — a sigh that hinted at an unutterable sadness — she changed the subject, as if the mere act of breathing out had dispelled her sorrow in a single puff. 'You want to be an official, don't you?' she asked after a brief pause.

'Yes, like every other soldier in the army.'

'Why? And don't tell me it's because you want to Serve the People or anything like that. I want to know the real reason.'

He hesitated. 'It'll make you angry.'

'It won't, I promise. I know you want your wife
to join you here.' She smiled a magnanimous smile.
'I'm your Sister, remember. I understand these
things. Don't worry, I'll help you. All promotions
are suspended at the moment but the minute things
start moving again I'll sort it out for your family.'
Her tears started up again, for no clear reason — as
if there were other things she wanted to say to him
but this was not the moment. She stood up and
went in search of a comb. 'What do you want to
eat?'

'I'll cook whatever you want,' he answered.

She smiled. 'I'm your wife, remember. I'll cook
whatever *you* want.'

Then down the stairs they went, hand in hand,
to prepare lunch. In the kitchen, they both immediately spotted the Serve the People! sign lying on
the table, and smiled. 'Serve the People,' he said.
'Sit down and rest.'

'Fight Selfishness and Criticize Revisionism,' she
replied. 'Sit down and rest yourself.'

'We've Come Together for a Common Revolutionary Goal,' he countered back. 'Let's cook together.'

'The People,' she concluded, 'and the People Alone, are the Driving Force of History. Let's make a competition of it, to find out who's the better cook.'

Between them, they produced two meat and two vegetable dishes: Liu Lian worked on cucumber with scrambled egg, and green pepper with diced pork, while he made stewed chicken and stir-fried aubergines. After each had sampled the other's, she declared hers superior, while he championed his. She was from south China, she argued, it stood to reason she would cook better than a rough northerner. He'd won second place in an army cookery competition, he countered; the Division Commander had chosen him for his culinary prowess. She flashed a mysterious smile at him. 'The meek will inherit the Revolution,' she said, as if conceding partial defeat. 'I'll award you a narrow victory in the main course. But wait until you've tried my soup.' She then prepared a soup of dried shrimps and stewed white gourd.

'The Eyes of the Masses are Indeed Bright,' he admitted, after tasting it. 'This is something special, better than anything I could do.'

Afterwards, they sat opposite each other to eat, their legs and feet touching and intertwining under the table. The meal quickly became a game as, laughing, they took turns to feed each other mouthfuls. Halfway through, Liu Lian struck her forehead, as if she'd suddenly remembered something terribly important. 'Have you ever tasted mao-tai?' she asked. He'd seen the senior officers drink it at this very table, he replied, the night he cooked a banquet—eight hot dishes and four cold—to celebrate the country's first successful nuclear explosion.

'Come on,' she said, 'let's have some. After all, we've got something to celebrate, too.'

'What's that?'

'Your making my life worthwhile.'

She went upstairs and fetched, from who knows where, a bottle of mao-tai—the finest, costliest of all Chinese spirits—and two cups. She filled both to the brim, passed one to him and raised hers as if about to toast him. He paused and looked across at her. 'If I drink this, you have to tell me the story of how you came to marry the Division Commander.'

A blank look passed over her face. 'You really want to know? All right. As long as you drink up first.'

'Promise?'

'I promise,' she replied.

He lifted his cup and drank. 'Where are you from in the south?'

'Yangzhou,' she answered, after draining her own cup. 'Ever been? You northerners are always saying how wonderful Hangzhou and Suzhou are, but Yangzhou's better than both. The girls are much prettier. Apparently, when they were looking for concubines for Deputy Head-of-State Lin Biao, they ignored Suzhou and Hangzhou completely, and chose two from Yangzhou instead.' As she spoke, she refilled both cups and passed his back to him. 'Anything else?'

'Did the Division Commander choose you, too?'

She swallowed her wine down. 'Of course. It was when he was on an inspection tour of the hospital. He picked me out straightaway.' Her radiant smile showed how proud she'd been that the Commander had noticed her. At the same moment, however, tears began to splash from her eyes and into her cup.

'What's wrong?' he asked.

'I'm happy. Happy I married the Division Commander.'

'Didn't you know how much older he was?' he asked.

'Yes.'

'And you still married him?'

'He's the Division Commander.'

'But he's impotent.'

'Don't say what you shouldn't say.'

'I'm your husband, I can say anything I want.'

'You're the Division Commander's orderly, and I'm his wife — remember?'

He slammed his wine cup down on the table, glaring at her. 'I don't know why,' he said, a sudden, solemn urgency in his voice, 'but just then the thought of you wanting to marry the Commander made me want to throttle you.'

She drank another cupful. 'Go on then,' she challenged him. 'We all have to die sometime, so we might as well go together.' Gulping another cup down, she looked in Wu Dawang's direction, already half-tipsy. 'I'm one of the Party faithful, too, you know. I knew more quotations by Chairman Mao than anyone else in the Division Hospital. Once, I recited a hundred of them to the Commander, one after the other. I was word-perfect. I even recited the punctuation. I think that's when he really took a shine to me. First promotion, then marriage. I was perfectly willing to marry him, truly I was, he didn't need to push me in the slightest. But it had never crossed my mind he'd be impotent, or that his first wife had divorced him because of it. Just when I was about to tell him I wanted a divorce, too, he kneeled in front of me. Imagine it! At his age, his rank. He joined the Communists to fight against the Japanese when he was only fourteen. He'd been wounded four times by 1945. Then, during the Civil War, he took a bullet between his legs. He's still got two bullets in him, one in his back, one in his knee. He's got a whole cupboard stuffed with medals and honours. How could I divorce him? A man who'd given every-thing for the Revolution, kneeling in front of me, crying like a baby?

'Come on,' she continued. 'If you drink up, I'll recite a hundred quotations by Chairman Mao. If you don't, I'll have a hundred from you.'

'I'd rather hear one of his songs,' he said.

'All right.' Once his cup was empty, she sang 'The Morning Sun'. Another cup later, she sang 'The Long March'. After another, 'Self-Reliance'. Soon, the tally of how many cups had been drunk and how many songs had been sung was lost in a drunken haze. When they woke, dusk was falling over the compound. The evening sun shone in through the kitchen window, illuminating a scene of near-orgiastic debauchery: the table scattered with cups, dishes and an empty bottle, the chairs piled with clothes, the floor strewn with chopsticks — one pair having inexplicably ended up behind the kitchen door.

Our hero and heroine lay, their arms wrapped around each other, on the cement floor of the kitchen, as nakedly pinkish-white as two pigs tossed by their butcher under his slaughter table. The Serve the People! sign lay unaccountably across their bodies, like a price tag.

VIII

HAD LIFE BEEN A GAME all along, or had it only
recently become one? Is all the world a stage, the men
and women on it merely players? Does passion come
from love, or can love come from passion? Does it
matter? A river doesn't need to know its source; the
source doesn't need to know what rivers it feeds—all
that matters is that it does so. In some instances, the
question of cause and effect is, ultimately, beside the
point. Some things—the love affair between Wu
Dawang and Liu Lian being one of them—seem to
come from nothing, then return to nothing.

As he worked in the back garden, she would
watch him—either from the kitchen doorway or
from the side of a vegetable patch, until her thoughts
began to wander when, say, a pair of butterflies fluttered languorously past. Blushing slightly, she would
go back inside, then re-emerge a few seconds later
holding the Serve the People! sign behind her back.

After setting it down a few feet away from him, she would turn back toward the house.

'Where are you going?' he would shout out.

'To get a drink of water,' she would reply. 'I'm thirsty.'

Not thinking to doubt her, he would carry on with his work until he discovered the sign. He would then look around him, throw down the hoe, take the sign back into the house, replace it on the dining table and, without pausing even to wash his hands or face, gallop upstairs to the bedroom where she would be undressed and waiting for him. No further communication was required. If he gave satisfaction, she would cook him whatever he felt like eating. If not, she would devise some domestic penalty for him. He ate what she cooked for him with an easy conscience, as easy as if he were the Division Commander eating food cooked by his Orderly; it was his reward for a job well done. Her punishments — washing her clothes, cleaning her ears, cutting her nails — he accepted just as easily, as fair penance for a selfish dereliction of duty. Love was a game to be played seriously. Once, she slipped the Serve the People! sign under his knife as he chopped vegetables in the kitchen. After he'd followed her upstairs, the smell of chilli still on his fingers, and given exceptional satisfaction, it was she who returned to the kitchen to pick up where he'd left off. In fact, she took over all the cooking for the next three days, not even allowing him to wash up afterward.

As the affair went on, the Serve the People! sign seemed to grow legs. An instant after she decided she wanted him, it would lodge itself in a blossoming shrub as he weeded a flower bed. Or, as he pruned the vines, it would suddenly appear hanging from a branch, nudging at his shoulder. While he was out shopping for food, the slightest thing could set him off on fantasies, which — on discovering the sign lying in wait for him back at Compound Number One — would swiftly become reality. Sometimes, of course, his thoughts would be elsewhere — with his wife and son, for example — but one glimpse of the sign obliterated everything except Liu Lian's glorious body and his desire for it. They would come together whenever and wherever: the sitting room, kitchen, bathroom, study, the Division Commander's conference room; even, under cover of darkness, beneath the vine trellis.

In a few short weeks, they'd become both the masters and slaves of instinct, allowing sex to dominate all other aspects of life. Between them, they could make the sexual act simple one minute, elaborate the next; now perfunctory, now ceremonious; now civilized, now decadent; now relaxed, now painstaking. But it was not until their last week together that their affair attained a truly extraordinary, climactic intensity.

Shortly before this, the Division had left on camp and field training. For days, trucks loaded with firewood, coal, clothes and grain had been parked in front of each company barracks. The poems, essays and lists of commendations that usually filled noticeboards had given way to posters urging their readers to Prepare for War and Natural Disasters, to Dig Holes That Are Deep and Amass Grain Stores That Are Large; to Triumph over US Imperialism and Soviet Revisionism on the Path to Victory in World War III, while constantly bearing in mind that Hegemony Must Not Be Sought. Battle challenges were exchanged; councils of war proposed. As slogan piled upon slogan, so the entire Division worked itself up into a revolutionary frenzy. Tucked away in the Division Commander's compound, Wu Dawang had almost forgotten what it was to be a soldier; how a single spark of propaganda could set the barracks alight. On the day of the Division's departure, he was pushing his bicycle out of Compound Number One after almost a week spent exclusively behind its reinforced steel fence, en route to market, when suddenly, what looked like the entire Division jogged past him in full battle dress toward the drill ground.

His body tensed with the nervous excitement of mobilization. 'What's going on?' he asked the sentry.

'Camp and field training,' came the reply. 'Haven't you heard?'

Without pausing to answer, he cycled quickly over to his barracks, where he discovered that his whole company — bar a skeleton staff left behind to look after the pigs and the vegetable garden — had left the evening before. He was told that his company had been sent off as an advance party, but the Captain and Political Instructor had issued him with a permit to stay. Retrieving it from the office, Wu Dawang saw it contained only one sentence: 'Your task is to remember at all times that to serve the Division

Commander's family is to Serve the People.' The instruction hit him like cold water in the face, filling him with a sense of unhappy abandonment.

Midsummer was now past. Though the dry heat persisted, its roasting intensity had gone, tempered by an edge of coolness that signalled autumn was not far off. After folding up the permit, Wu Dawang rode resentfully on to market, filled his baskets with chicken, fish, peanut oil, sesame oil, MSG and ground pepper for the house, then went on to the post office to send thirty *yuan* back home.

In the normal run of things, he was in the habit of posting seven or eight *yuan* back home at the end of each month, to help with the housekeeping. And yet here he was, sending money long before the end of the month, and much more than usual. This was one of the few blots—blacker even than his adulterous liaison with his supreme superior's wife—on Wu Dawang's otherwise unsullied army record. The year he joined the army, at a little over twenty-two years old, he'd received six *yuan* as a monthly allowance, the second year seven, the third eight and so on, enjoying an increase of one *yuan* each year. Five years on, he still received only ten *yuan*, every cent of which — beyond the one or two *yuan* he spent each month on toothpaste and soap — he sent back home. How he'd managed to save up the staggering sum of thirty *yuan* was therefore information he was anxious to keep classified.

He'd scrimped the money together from odds and ends of petty cash — only cents, not whole *yuan* — left over from the food shopping he did for the Division Commander's household. Although he knew this was no hanging offence, Wu Dawang was aware that embezzlement — however minor — was still embezzlement. As a result, whenever he bought anything he would up the price by one or two cents on the official record. His accounts were thus never anything less than perfectly square, for which both the Commander and Liu Lian had commended him. This thirty *yuan* now in transit to his wife was the culmination of months of careful planning and scheming. It went some way toward relieving his troubled marital conscience, enabling him to pursue his recklessly passionate affair with Liu Lian with a lighter heart.

As he left the post office, the sun shining bright in a cloudless sky, a file of troops was marching along the main street, waving flags and banners and shouting abusive slogans at some new enemy of the state. After a month of the cloistered, underground existence he'd been leading with Liu Lian, the raw, revolutionary zeal of everyday life now struck him as unfamiliar, even alarming. He stood at the side of the street, watching, as if trying to work out whether the demonstration was in any way an attack on his degenerate entanglement with the Division Commander's wife. When, at last, the marchers had passed noisily on, he set off again on his bike.

By the time he arrived back, the Division was long gone. Only the lonely footsteps of the relief patrol echoed up and down the road that cut through the deserted barracks. Although the sparrows and cicadas were no louder or more numerous than before, their voices now seemed to reverberate deafeningly across the drill ground. Marching up and down, the patrols left behind now struck him as oddly unconvincing, as if they were playacting, the guns on their shoulders no more intimidating than flags or placards. As Wu Dawang approached the Division Commander's gate, a careless sparrow happened to shit on his cap, an event duly reported to him by the compound sentry from his duty platform. Wu Dawang paused, still holding on to his bicycle. 'Do you know who I am?' he asked irritably. 'I'm the company's Model Soldier. How dare you speak to me like that?'

'I know who you are, Sergeant Wu,' the sentry replied. 'But there really is shit on your cap.'

As soon as he'd taken off his cap to see for himself, Wu Dawang smiled and wiped it off. 'I'm the Division Commander's Orderly. Just let me know if there's anything you need help with.' Saying these few simple words made Wu Dawang's heart fairly sing with happiness, because the sentry thanked him for them as profusely as he would have the Division Commander himself.

In fact, since the start of his affair with Liu Lian, a subtle, psychological change had been taking place in Wu Dawang: sometimes he would catch himself imagining he was indeed Liu Lian's husband, the master of the household he served. Many times he had felt a secret, boastful urge to divulge to others some of the details of his relationship with Liu Lian. Only his revolutionary self-discipline — together with the fact that no one would have believed him, and the impossibility of guaranteeing his confidant's discretion—had so far sealed his lips.

As Wu Dawang wheeled his bike around to the back door, some of this new complacency must have shown on his face and in his manner, unwittingly triggering a startling new turn to their affair. Throwing his purchases into the kitchen, he glimpsed Liu Lian coming in the front door, carrying a few everyday toiletries—toothpaste, soap, powder, face-cream, and so on. When she reached the doorway to the dining room, she glanced over at the Serve the People! sign on the dining table. But, just as she opened her mouth to speak, Wu Dawang tugged off his sweaty uniform and held it out to her. 'Go and give that a wash.'

She stared at him. 'What did you just say?'

'I'm boiling hot,' he said. 'Wash my clothes.'

His tone was precisely the one he would have used with his wife, expecting her to wash and cook for him when he came in from the fields. He was not, however, speaking to his wife. Displeasure flashed across Liu Lian's face. Ignoring the uniform, she pointed silently at the Serve the People!

sign, a faint jeer about her mouth. She then turned toward the shower room, her toiletries still cradled in her arms.

From the kitchen, Wu Dawang had an uninterrupted view of the sign. Though its text and images had been tarnished by cooking smoke, its message still chimed across at Wu Dawang like an alarm bell, reminding him of the role he'd been assigned to play in Compound Number One, of the inferior status that a peasant soldier could shake off only in his fantasies.

He slowly retracted his hand and uniform. Squatting down onto his heels like a deflated leather ball, he let his clothes fall to the ground. He gazed out of the back door, into the vegetable garden. At one side stood a small copse of poplars, their trunks cracked open into fissured knots that stared back at him. The colour drained from his face, he turned back to the Serve the People! sign, then sprang up and ran to the shower room. No Liu Lian. He pounded up the stairs to the bathroom where he discovered her dabbing her face with some of the powder she'd just bought. Charging in, he gathered her up in his arms and began staggering off with her toward the bedroom. In the confusion of this hasty manoeuvre, and as she was struggling to free herself, she knocked a framed scarlet and yellow quotation by the Chairman off the wall. A second later, he accidentally trod on it, shattering the glass and embellishing the Great Truth beneath ('Without a People's Army, the People Have Nothing') with a large, dusty footprint.

A stunned silence fell.

He put her down. They looked at the smashed quotation, then at each other.

'What the hell have you done?' she demanded.

'You were the one who knocked it off the wall.'

She looked down at his footprint. 'One call to Security and you're a dead man.'

'Is that what you're going to do?'

She glanced at his stricken face. 'I might. And I might not.'

His voice became more cajoling. 'You were the one who made me come upstairs. If you hadn't, it wouldn't have fallen off the wall, would it?'

Liu Lian looked at him like a mother would at a son who'd just slapped her. As she stared hard at him, her expression of startled uncertainty changed into shocked indignation. 'What did you just say?'

'I said, it was you who made me come upstairs.'

'When?'

'Just now, in the kitchen, when you pointed at the Serve the People! sign.'

She laughed drily. She had meant to remind him of the sign's literal meaning, of his real status in the house, but he had chosen to understand only the private sexual code they had devised for it; to serve her according to less conventional Communist principles. She had no idea what had passed through Wu Dawang's head as he'd squatted, staring out at the garden, that a long-hidden resentment at the rigid hierarchy all around him was about to burst forth. As she contemplated his simple, honest face, compassion welled up inside her. She felt she'd treated him unfairly. She placed his hand on her breast, as if to comfort him, and traced her own soft, slender finger across the back of it. This familiar, affectionate gesture offered Wu Dawang first sexual encouragement, then opened the floodgates to his suppressed, unarticulated feelings of discontent. With reckless abandon, he scooped her up in his arms, carried her over to the bed—further trampling the Chairman's quotation underfoot—threw her down on it and began roughly undressing her.

She lay on her back, both legs in the air, submitting to this unceremonious treatment. As he entered her, he was overcome by a new kind of happiness — a triumphant sense of taking revenge for some past wrong, of getting the better of an oppressor. The strange thing, though, was that, far from outraging her, this almost animal outburst of his seemed to be giving her just as much pleasure. Her startlingly loud, raw, uninhibited sobs urged him on until, finally victorious in his complete possession of her, he collapsed to the ground at the foot of the bed, naked and dripping with sweat. The fragments of glass and damaged quotation lay around him like rubbish.

She lay quietly on the bed, also naked except for a pillow pulled over her thighs. Both stared, unmoving, up at the ceiling, sunk in postcoital anticlimax.

The midday sun poured in through the window, illuminating golden stars of airborne dust. While the songs of sparrows and turtledoves clattered around them, the cicadas sounded hoarse, exhausted, their voices dying away almost as soon as they'd made themselves heard. They lay there in silence, letting the time pass between them, a sense of extraordinary fatigue hanging in the air.

'What time is it?' she eventually asked, still without moving, as if the ceiling might supply the answer.

'I don't know,' he replied, also to the ceiling. 'Are you hungry?' he asked.

'No. Wu Dawang, we've become animals.'

'I don't care.'

'Where did all that come from?'

'All what?'

'All that just now.'

'I feel like I'm full of hatred, inside. Somehow, just then, it all came out.'

'Who do you hate?'

'I don't know.'

'Is it me?'

'No, I don't think so.'

'I feel like that, too.'

'Who do you hate?'

'I'm not sure either.'

She sat up and put her clothes on, then lay back down on the bed. 'There's no one around,' she said. 'I wish we could spend the rest of our lives locked in here together.'

'When's the Commander back?'

'Don't worry yourself about that. But the minute he is, I'll get him to fix your promotion.'

'At the very least, let's lock ourselves in here for a full three days and three nights before he comes back. Then, when he does, I'll go back to my company. Whatever happens, I can't stay here.'

'Why not?'

'D'you think I could face him after everything that's happened between us?'

A silence spun out between them, as he waited to hear what she thought would happen between the two of them when the Division Commander came home. Instead, she eventually asked him: 'What did you buy in town?'

He told her about the food he'd bought.

'How long will that last us?' she wanted to know next.

'Over a month.'

She sat up and combed a hand through her tangled hair. Standing up, she glanced down at his naked body. Then she wandered, smiling, downstairs.

When he heard her go outside, he picked himself up from the floor and went across to the window. He saw her walk over to the entrance to the compound with an iron lock in her hands, check to left and right that no soldiers were approaching along the road, and pull the two iron gates shut. Putting her hands through the gates, she padlocked them together on the outside to give the illusion that no one was at home. Returning to the house, she locked both front and back doors.

The stage was now set for the culminating seventy-two hours of their affair. He dressed while he waited for her. By the time she reappeared, however, she'd already taken off all her clothes again. They stood facing each other across the bedroom doorway.

'I've locked everything up,' she said.

'We haven't much rice,' he replied.

'I've checked. There's still half a bag in the cupboard.'

'That should be enough.'

'Why have you put your clothes back on?'

He undressed again, folding his uniform carefully away in her wardrobe as if he planned never to put it back on.

FOR THREE DAYS AND THREE nights, Liu Lian and Wu Dawang imprisoned themselves within the house, attending only to their most primitive needs. The compound began to seem like a wholly autonomous domain, answerable only to its own laws, independent of the world beyond its steel fence. They came together whenever and however they wanted, and when they were tired they rested as they were — sitting or lying, his head resting on her thigh, prickling her tender skin with its bristly crew cut — until their energies returned.

But after a certain point — on the afternoon of the third day — primitive joy gave way to primitive fatigue; a fatigue that was not only physical, but also psychological.

The position of the Division Commander's house, within the senior officers' compound, made it easy to keep their wanton confinement hidden. Over the road in front of the compound was the back wall of the Division Social Club. With the barracks deserted, the gate to the club was permanently locked. Its gongs, drums and more exotic musical instruments (an exultant French horn, a dazzling bronze flute and a set of huge scarlet timpani, wheeled out only for the promulgation of Chairman Mao's highest directives, for important conferences in Beijing or for great matters of state) were all deathly silent. Even if the gate was thrown open and the drums brought back to life, much of the noise would have been muffled by its thick red-brick walls; only a faint, indistinct rumble would disturb the peace of the Commander's house. Likewise, anyone in the club would be oblivious to noise generated by Wu Dawang and Liu Lian.

The vegetable garden and a copse of willows screened the back of the house from the headquarters of the Signals Company. Neither had ever heard anything of the other's existence.

To the east was an abandoned building site. The Division Commander's predecessor had planned a recreational conference facility for the senior officers, in which they could read the papers, chat, play chess or ping-pong, and so on, after dinner. And when it came to meetings, of course, the conference room would only be a few steps from their front doors. But one evening, shortly after the current Division Commander had been appointed, he stood surveying the construction site, studying the lie of the land and inviting opinions from a few of his immediate subordinates. 'In the words of Chairman Mao,' he finally pronounced, 'work is like a carrying-pole lying on the ground before us, testing us as to whether or not we dare take it onto our shoulders. Sometimes the load is heavy, and sometimes it is light. Some eagerly grasp the light load but fear the heavy, pushing it on to the shoulders of others. This is an example of incorrect thinking. Some comrades, by contrast, delight in taking up the heavy loads for themselves and leaving the light work to others, in putting themselves last and others first. This is the good Communist spirit which we all need to emulate.'

His recitation complete, the Division Commander went back to his house to drink the after-dinner tea his new wife Liu Lian had prepared for him. From that moment on, the building work ground to a vigorous halt and the site was overrun by scrubby weeds. The sentries only patrolled on the other side of the red-brick wall that skirted the site — well away from the house itself. The inhabitants of Compound Number One would need to be screaming blue murder to be overheard by the patrols. Only to the west was the house overlooked — by Compound Number Two, the Political Commissar's house. As luck would have it, though, with the Commissar off on camp and field training, his wife had gone on social manoeuvres to the provincial capital, taking her orderly with her on a tour of her relatives.

All was as if Heaven itself had willed it. And, true to this Heaven-sent opportunity, for the first two and a half days they remained inside the house, enslaving themselves to their most basic desires. In the end, though, their weary bodies let them down, refusing them more of the same delirious happiness. Even though they tried the exact position that had worked so ecstatically well — her lying on her back on the bed, him standing at its foot — success eluded them. They considered endless permutations and variations of arrangement and mood; none had the desired effect.

Failure trailed them, like a shadow.

'What's wrong?' she asked, as they lay exhausted on the bed.

'I'm just tired,' he replied.

'It's not that. You're bored with me.'

'I want to put some clothes on and go and do some work in the garden. I'll get undressed again when I come back inside, all right?'

'Please yourself.'

He climbed down off the bed and went over to her wardrobe. However, as he opened the door, an accident of incalculable counter-revolutionary enormity occurred—one that threatened the very fabric of society and state; something far more serious than stamping on one of Chairman Mao's quotations. Taking his uniform out of the wardrobe, he brought with it a plaster statue of Mao Zedong. It plummeted to the ground and shattered pitilessly all over the floor, filling the room with powdery shards. Chairman Mao's severed head rolled, just as a ping-pong ball would, over to the side of the table, discarding en route its snow-white nose, which came to rest, like a dust-covered soya bean, in the middle of the room.

Wu Dawang stood white-faced, rooted to the spot, as the smell of plaster of Paris billowed up around him.

With a squeal of alarm, Liu Lian bolted from the bed and to the telephone. 'Hello, switchboard?' she gabbled into the receiver. 'Is the Head of Security still in barracks?'

In an instant, Wu Dawang understood the gravity of the situation. The word 'bitch' springing disbelievingly to his lips, he dropped his uniform and charged over to grab the telephone from Liu Lian.

'What the hell are you doing?' he barked, slamming it back down.

She concentrated on struggling free and getting the receiver back. To stop her, he stood guard in front of the table, repelling all her desperate, violent lunges, swatting her arms away, muttering angrily beneath his breath. He was amazed by her strength and stamina: every time he saw her off, she would somehow return for a fresh assault. At last, to get her away from the telephone, he gathered her up to his chest — much as one would capture a large bird by wrapping one's arms around it — carried her to the bed and threw her contemptuously down onto it. He then trampled very deliberately over the bits of plaster, grinding them to dust, as he repeated over and over to her and to himself: 'Still think you're going to make that phone call? Think you're going to go running to Security?' He placed his bare foot on the Chairman's head and twisted it down, hard. 'You heartless bitch,' he said again, staring at Liu Lian as he twisted it back the other way. When he'd reduced everything beneath his feet to powder, he realized—rather to his surprise—that he hadn't heard her say a single thing through this entire violent outburst of his. Taking a moment to look more calmly at her, he discovered that, far from seeming traumatized by the political cataclysm of the last few minutes, she was sitting serenely on the edge of the bed, gazing at him, her cheeks flushed and eyes shining with anticipation.

Glancing down at himself, he realized that their violent, naked struggle had reawoken in him that elusive sense of furious excitement. For some reason, the way she was gazing almost wonderingly at him—as a tourist might gawp at a jumping, squawking monkey in a zoo—only intensified his rage at her ruthless attempt to betray him. Roughly, he turned her onto her front and entered her from behind, pouring—just as he had done three days earlier—all his desire for revenge into this intense sexual impulse.

Again, as she had done three days ago, she burst into loud, happy sobs.

When she'd regained her composure, she turned over, slid off the bed and came to squat, smiling, down next to him. 'I put that statue under your clothes. I knew that as soon as you tried to get dressed, you'd knock it to the ground.'

Discovering he'd been tricked, he might have grabbed hold of her hair—perhaps to hit her, or just to shout at her, to express his anger. Instead, he took her ravishingly pretty face in his hands and kissed it. 'I didn't mean it when I called you a bitch just then.'

She shook her head at him, her face pink with gratitude. Outside, after some light drizzle, the sun was coming back out into an almost clear sky, filling the room with the mellow, golden light of approaching autumn. She stood up and sat, straight backed, on the bed once more. A modest glint of triumph lit up her face, her beatific smile sharpened by a kind of knowing, feminine mischief.

A deep quiet fell over the room, as if the physical world around them had dissolved into nothingness. The sweat steamed off their bodies, adding a salty tang to the room's musty air.

They gazed at each other, both their faces suddenly wet with tears. It was as if this unhinged passion had, somewhere deep inside their numbed psyches, awoken a capacity for love of which neither had known they were capable; a love that both knew could only end in painful separation. Neither dared say or do anything, for fear it would bring their fragile, unsustainable liaison instantly to an end. Their tears pattered onto the ground, like raindrops falling from eaves. He took a step forward and, kneeling before her, laid his head on her lap like a child looking for comfort. As she distractedly ran a finger through his short hair, her tears fell onto his face, mingling with his own before running down her legs. She tilted his face up toward her and kissed him, as a prelude to speaking.

'Would you like to marry me?'

'Yes.'

'I'd like to marry you, too, but it's impossible.'

His eyes asked why.

'Have you forgotten who my husband is?'

She spoke mildly, without emphasis; as if talking about some trivial object she had absentmindedly lost. But to him her words sounded like a warning. His tears stopped, cut off at the source. At the same time the gentle sorrow in her expression stiffened into awkward reserve, as if Wu Dawang were a passing stranger she'd mistaken for a friend.

'So you don't want to leave the Commander?' he said.

'Of course I do. But it's not going to happen.'

'Why not?'

'Because he's the Division Commander.'

'Didn't his last wife divorce him?'

'More fool her.'

'So you don't want to leave him?' he repeated.

'Look, I'm not going to ask him for a divorce. I'm just happy that you want to marry me; that's enough for me. And I'll keep my promise: I'll do whatever it takes to get you your promotion and have your family moved to the city. Whatever you want, I'll make sure you get it.'

Though their eyes were now dry, neither had noticed when the other had stopped crying; when the great tide of love had begun to ebb. Reality had conquered fantasy. Wu Dawang was neither particularly surprised by or inclined to doubt Liu Lian's resolve — from the outset, he'd known how the thing would turn out. But for a brief instant he'd allowed a delusion to overwhelm his common sense. Neither suspected the other of shedding insincere tears; both knew that, sooner or later, hard truth would prevail over daydreams.

None the less, Wu Dawang became almost petulant in his desperation to retrieve that fleeting, shared intensity of feeling from the clutches of Liu Lian's cool pragmatism. Retreating a few steps, he sat down on the chair by the table.

'I don't care whether you divorce the Commander, fix me a promotion or get my family moved to the city. Whatever happens, I'll never forget you.'

This declaration didn't have the impact he'd anticipated. After a pause, Liu Lian merely smiled. 'Flatterer.'

Wu Dawang's face crumpled anxiously. 'Don't you believe me?'

'Of course. Like I believe Chairman Mao's really going to live for 10,000 years,' she teased.

He cast about for a way of proving his devotion. Finally, his eyes fell on the dust of the statue that he'd first smashed to pieces, then crushed to powder underfoot. 'If you don't believe me,' he said, 'you can tell Security what I did to that statue. I'll either be shot or spend the rest of my life in prison.'

He kicked again at the powder dusted over the floor, his face sweating with agitation. When he looked back up, she was still contemplating him — but more seriously than before.

'Do you really think I'm going to forget you?'

'You're the Division Commander's wife, you can forget whoever you like. All I know is I'll never forget you.'

'D'you want me to swear it?'

'Hot air.'

Glancing across at the poster of Chairman Mao stuck above the table, she walked over, ripped it off the wall, screwed it up and tore it into pieces. She then threw them onto the floor and stamped on them.

'You can report me, too. Once we were both Party-faithful. Now we're both counterrevolutionaries. But you destroyed an image of Chairman Mao by accident, while I did it deliberately. Which makes me more counterrevolutionary. Believe me now?'

For a moment he paled with shock at what she'd done. Then he walked over to the basin, pulled a quotation off the wall behind it and, like her, screwed it up and stamped on it.

'I'm more counterrevolutionary than you. I deserve two firing squads.'

Scanning the room, her eyes fixed on a red book lying on the corner of the writing table: *The Selected Works of Mao Zedong*. She grabbed up the bible of Revolution, pulled off its jacket and tossed it to the ground, then tore through its pages, ripping and screwing them up until finally she reached the title page with its portrait of Chairman Mao, which she made into a ball and stamped on.

'Now who's the bigger counterrevolutionary?'

Without replying, he strode out of the room and over to the stairwell. There, he threw onto the floor the framed double portrait of Lin Biao and Chairman Mao entitled *The Great Helmsman Guides Us Across the Seas*. Having smashed the glass, he gouged out the two men's eyes into four dark, scowling holes. He then straightened up and looked over at her. 'You tell me.'

She walked into the Division Commander's map-filled conference room and staggered back out carrying an almost life-sized, gold-plated bust of Chairman Mao. After laying the statue down in front of Wu Dawang she chiselled off its nose with a neat little hammer. 'How about that, then?'

From the ground floor, he brought up a Chairman Mao badge and a nail, then hammered the latter through the nose of the former. His work done, he stared defiantly at her.

She, too, went downstairs. Finding a medicine cabinet with the Chairman's face printed on it, she hammered two large nails through its eyes.

Over a quotation stamped on to a washbowl — 'Fight Selfishness, Criticize Revisionism' — he scribbled 'Please Yourself'.

She found two enamel army mugs, both emblazoned with Mao quotations and portraits. After smearing the text and pictures with ink, she threw both cups into the large ceramic basin she used as a bidet.

They searched out every single item—every picture, bowl, vessel, cabinet or chair—that had any link to Mao Zedong and the Great Men of the Revolution, and destroyed or defaced them all. After making sure the sitting room had been stripped bare of its revolutionary memorabilia, Liu Lian ran into the kitchen and smashed every rice bowl decorated with images of Mao.

Wu Dawang broke a brand-new aluminium pot covered in the Chairman's quotations.

When the cupboards refused to yield up any more holy objects for desecration, she proceeded into the dining room and seized the talismanic Serve the People! sign that had borne near-constant witness to their affair. However, as she lifted it up to smash it, he strode over, wrested it from her and placed it carefully back on the table.

'What are you doing?' she asked.

'I want to keep it.'

'What for?'

'I just do.'

'First you have to admit that I am the greatest counterrevolutionary the world has ever known, a poisonous viper hidden in the breast of the Party and a devastating time bomb ticking away deep in the ranks of the Revolution. And finally, that I love you a hundred times more than you love me.'

'Do I have to?'

'I'll smash it if you don't.'

'All right, I admit it.'

'Say it three times.'

Three times he admitted she was the greatest counterrevolutionary the world has ever known, a poisonous viper hidden in the breast of the Party and a devastating time bomb ticking away deep in the ranks of the Revolution. He then went on to say, again three times, that her love for him exceeded his for her a hundred, a thousand, ten thousand times.

They gazed at each other, tears shining in their eyes.

As dusk cast its hazy, grubby light through the downstairs, the evening breeze brought a refreshing coolness to the house. While they stood listening to the music of the birds returning to their nests, surveying their surroundings, there was an almost mystical quality to the quiet that had descended after their riotous frenzy of destruction.

Just as the silence between them was beginning to seem as interminable as *The Collected Works of Mao Zedong*, she wiped away her tears with her hand. 'I'm hungry,' she said.

He, too, wiped away his tears. 'Then I'll cook you something.'

'I'm thirsty.'

'Then I'll get you some water.'

'I'm cold.'

'Are you going to get dressed?'

'I'd rather die.'

'So what's to be done?'

She picked up the Serve the People! sign from the table.

He walked over and swept her up in his arms, as one would an exhausted child, then climbed slowly upstairs to the bedroom. The sound of his footsteps on the stairs, crunching the debris of their afternoon's work, echoed through the house like a wooden mallet striking a great empty drum.

THAT NIGHT, REINVIGORATED BY THE chaos they
had created, they found new heights of pleasure in
each other, before falling into a deep, exhausted sleep.
But hunger soon woke them again. With his usual iron
self-discipline, Wu Dawang forced his trembling legs
to carry him down to the kitchen to Serve the People.
Once there, however, he found there were no vegetables left. This discovery would require him to betray their solemn vow not to leave the house—a
transgression he viewed as seriously as the violation
of a religious oath. Fortunately, daylight was not far
from breaking after the final night of their three days'
self-imposed confinement. Thinking she'd gone back
to sleep, he decided not to risk disturbing her by fetch-
ing his clothes from the bedroom, and headed, still
naked, out into the vegetable garden.

Almost as soon as he'd opened the door, he felt the
moon—like an enormous piece of glass—gleaming

down at him from a cloudless sky of a pure, midnight blue. Its startling silver-white brilliance filled Wu Dawang with a familiar fear—that it might fall from the sky at any moment.

This was the third time in his life Wu Dawang had been seized by this anxiety. The first was the night his father passed away. The second was his wedding night, as the loveless reality of his marriage dawned upon him. He could not yet tell what it meant for him this time.

As he set off down the path through the vegetable garden, Wu Dawang felt overwhelmingly weary. His legs threatened to give way beneath him like straw. But despite his vague sense of moonlit foreboding Wu Dawang's dominant emotion at that moment was still one of happy fulfilment. What more could he hope for? For almost two months, he had lived with the beautiful wife of his Supreme Commander, a ranking officer in her own right, a Party zealot, a model of political correctness who knew *The Collected Works of Mao Zedong* as well as—better—than he did. Not only had she enabled him to enjoy the most exquisitely intense physical pleasures, but she had also promised to arrange the promotion that would en-

able his family to escape from that benighted wasteland of a village to the glorious city life that he craved
constantly — even in sleep. He was about to achieve
his very own paradise on earth.

Though he no longer felt as eager to be reunited
with his wife, the thought of his son — and their long
separation — filled him with impatience for the four-
pocketed official's jacket of thick green twill that
would mark the start of this new life of ease.

Two months ago, Wu Dawang had wanted this
promotion to make good his pledge to the Zhao
family. Now, however, he was motivated just as
powerfully by a desire to establish himself permanently in the army so that — after this rapturously
happy chapter in his life had drawn to an end — he
could at least still be close to Liu Lian. For soon
enough Wu Dawang would bid farewell to Compound Number One: to its vegetable garden, flower
bed, vine trellis and kitchen; to all the objects —
pots, bowls, ladles, dishes, chopsticks, vegetable
sacks — that bore no political messages, no quotations, no slogans, no images of Party leaders, and
that had therefore survived yesterday's orgy of
destruction. Worst of all, he would have to leave

his beloved Liu Lian. For now, he still had no sense
of how their parting would affect him, of how much
unhappiness lay ahead. Nor did he know that the
aftershocks from this love affair of his were about
to make themselves felt in unforeseen ways. He had
not learnt yet that fate is cyclical: that long periods
of calm succeed brief bursts of passionate intensity;
that moments of extreme happiness inevitably give
way to sorrow.

As Wu Dawang stood deep in thought, Liu Lian,
now dressed in a pair of pink panties and a cream
bra, came out into the garden and crept up behind
him. After watching him unnoticed for a while, she
slipped back into the house to fetch a rush mat, a
bag of biscuits and two glasses of water. This second time, she did not worry about disturbing him.
Her heavy footsteps startled him out of his covetous dreams and he turned to find her just behind
him.

As he sat down on a ridge of earth, he guiltily remembered the call of duty: that he was meant to be
cooking her something.

'I'm sorry, I forgot about the vegetables. Forgive
me.'

Liu Lian neither responded nor registered any displeasure. Her face remained calm, as if nothing had happened. While he'd been outside, she'd got herself in order: she'd bathed, combed her hair and powdered herself with the perfumed talc from Shanghai that in those days was within the reach of only a tiny minority of women. It seemed to Wu Dawang as if she'd left behind those three heart-stopping days and nights they had just spent together; as if their eight weeks of living almost as equals were drawing to a close. She was still the Division Commander's wife, the prettiest woman in the barracks, in the entire city even. Though she was dressed only in her underwear, his bedfellow of the past two months had somehow transformed back into a *grande dame* — still beguilingly young and beautiful, but a *grande dame* all the same. She walked to the middle of the cabbage patch, pulled up a handful of seedlings and threw them to one side. Unrolling the mat over the cleared ground, she put down the cups and biscuits, then glanced across at him.

'Come and have something to eat. There's something I want to tell you.'

He continued to wonder at the subtle physical
change that had come over her—a change that went
much deeper than the simple act of her putting some
clothes back on. Though he could not yet make sense
of it, something had happened. It was clear from the
new, quietly commanding tone of her voice alone.

He felt suddenly apprehensive—though whether
from fear of her, or of whatever it was that had happened, he could not say. He looked down at her, sitting there before him on the mat. 'Shall I get dressed?'

'No need.'

'You have.'

'Do you want me to get undressed again?'

Although that was more or less exactly what he
did want, he resisted saying so. In any case, in her
pink and cream underwear she was almost as fasci-
nating to him as when she was naked. He went over
and sat opposite her, deliberately assuming a child-
like pose, drawing both legs up to his chest to cover
his penis. She gave him a faint, slightly wounded
smile, like an older sister noticing her brother's first
physical shyness, then passed him some biscuits.

'Since we haven't much longer together, I ought
to serve you.'

They sat together, eating and drinking, the silver of the moonlight washing over the garden. When they'd finished, she brushed the crumbs off the mat, placed the empty cups under a nearby plant and looked up at the sky.

'I think I might be pregnant.'

Though he'd heard her clearly enough, he was unable at first to grasp the full implications of her announcement. After a brief pause, he asked her to repeat what she'd just said. Perhaps because she was surprised by the coolness of his reaction or because she was unwilling to confirm her revelation, Liu Lian merely narrowed her eyes at him, then tilted her head back to contemplate the moon, a glow of secret triumph on her face. A fresh, pungent smell was rising up from the ground: since he'd been locked away in the house, the onions and chives had started to bolt and the night air was now flavoured with their strong, hot scent.

As Wu Dawang noted to himself that the chives would become inedible if they were not cut back soon, the full complexity of Liu Lian's disclosure dawned on him. It had none of the simplicity of a political thought-crime; it was not something that could be rectified by a few years' hard labour. It was an emotional and biological event that broke down all the moral, social, cultural and political boundaries of their world. As the enormous consequence of her words reverberated through his mind, they all but cancelled out his happiness of just a few moments earlier. He repeated his question. 'What did you just say?'

'Nothing.'

'You just said you think you're pregnant.'

'I think I might be, but I don't feel like I am. Strong flavours don't make me feel sick. My period's due about now, but so far there's no sign of it. Maybe all that sex is making me late.'

Because she was so serene, so matter-of-fact, his anxieties were allayed. She shifted around so that she was directly opposite him, pulling her legs toward her, mirroring his own pose. She nudged the sole of his foot with her big toe; he returned the pressure. This friendly contact seemed to crack the reserve that had sprung up between them, restoring something of their old intimacy. But before Wu Dawang could relax back into his complacent euphoria, she lay down again and broached an even more serious issue.

'Lie down next to me, I want to ask you a few things. And you have to answer truthfully.'

'Ask away.'

'Lie down first.'

He lay down shoulder to shoulder with her. Because he was feeling calm again, he could savour the sensory pleasures of reclining next to her: her soft, smooth skin caressing his muscular shoulder like a trickle of water; the sweet, ripe-apple scent of her talcum powder. He was surprised by his sudden, heightened awareness of this fragrance, which he'd become almost desensitized to over the weeks. It seemed somehow to have dissolved into the dew, taking on an almost tangible intensity, settling over the plants and into the soil, mixing with the lingering sharpness of the earth itself.

He climbed on top of her. 'I want you,' he implored.

'Get off me a minute. I need to ask you something.'

He climbed back off her and lay his head on her bosom, his right ear on her right breast.

She moved his head down to her stomach.

'Will you be afraid,' she asked gravely, 'if I really am pregnant?'

'No.'

'Won't you be afraid of the Division Commander finding out?'

'I want him to find out.'

'But what'll happen to you if he does?'

'At worst, he'll have me sent to prison. As long as they don't shoot me, I can marry you when I get out.'

'Marry? How?'

'If he finds out, surely the Commander won't want you anymore. Then we can get married.'

She chose not to respond to the scenario he'd sketched out—or to the question of whether the Division Commander would still want her after he'd found out about their affair. Instead she raised instead another, equally fundamental issue.

'Would you be willing to divorce your wife?'

'Yes. So long as you moved her and my son to the city and fixed her up with a steady job and my son with a school.'

She sat up. 'And if I couldn't?'

He sat up, too. 'I promised before I married her, I swore an oath. You'd have to.'

'But what if—what if I couldn't?'

'Of course you can. No question. As long as she gets her life in the city, I'll have done my duty by her. I'll divorce whenever you want and marry as soon as you'll have me. Even if the Commander throws you out, you ask me to get a divorce and then decide I'm not good enough for you — and I know I'm not good enough for you — I'll still stand by you. I won't marry anyone else, or have anything to do with my ex-wife. Any time you need me, all you need to do is write or phone and I'll come straight to you.'

Having said his piece, he looked across at her expectantly, like a child handing his homework in to his teacher.

From a few inches away, she stared hard back at him, trying to gauge his sincerity by the light of the moon. Unable to detect a flicker of flippancy in him, she kissed him passionately, then removed her clothes and hung them on a nearby plant. Turning back to him, she spoke of a sterner, more inescapable reality.

'The Division Commander's coming back earlier than expected — today in fact, so these are our last few hours together. For weeks now, you've done everything for me. It'll be light soon, so let me serve you for the time we've got left—anything you want, anything to make you happy. I want you to remember me for the rest of your life.'

Beneath the steadiness of her voice, Wu Dawang could sense her sadness. The moon had glided east of the barracks, and a distinct chill had descended over the garden, turning Liu Lian's skin bluish-white and covering her shoulders and arms with goose bumps. But it was the news of the Division Commander's imminent return, not the fall in temperature that made Wu Dawang shiver.

She stretched out beside him again.

He looked at her with the same detachment that one might consider a portrait, until the composition before him began to swim out of focus, its lines blurring. As she lay there waiting for him, Liu Lian's breathing quickened slightly—with impatience. But he stayed where he was, holding her hand, as if he was afraid of losing her. Suddenly, without knowing why, tears welled up in his eyes. In all the time they'd been together, she'd always been the first of the two of them to cry. From the very start he had, of course, known how the thing would end—with the Commander's return. None the less, the news that this ending was scheduled for the day ahead still struck him as hurtfully sudden.

'Has the Commander rung?'

'Didn't you hear the phone just now?'

He hadn't. The telephone had in fact rung several times over the past eight weeks, and not once had he wondered what Liu Lian had said to her husband, what lies she'd stalled him with. Thanks to his slavish devotion to duty — Don't Ask What You Shouldn't Ask, Don't Listen To What You Shouldn't Listen To, Don't Say What You Shouldn't Say — he'd been able to block this question out entirely, saving himself from any number of extra anxieties. Now, however, that their return to reality was only hours away, he had no choice but to face up to his present situation.

'I want to go home, Liu Lian.'

'When?'

'Before the Division Commander gets back.'

She sat up and put her arms around him, resting her head on his shoulder. 'Are you afraid? You've no need to be, while I'm here. I'll make sure everything's settled. It'll be as if nothing had ever happened.' But as soon as she'd offered these words of comfort, she immediately seemed to change her mind. 'Then again, maybe it would be best if you did go away for a bit, to spend some time with your family. I'll fix you up with some leave. Stay at home until your company recalls you.'

A slow trail of footsteps rang out along the road: first approaching, then retreating into the distance, and eventually fading into silence. They both followed the sound with their eyes, recognizing the tread of the relief patrol. When all was quiet once more, their thoughts returned to their predicament.

'How will I live without you, Liu Lian?'

'How will *I* live without *you*?' Both, by this point, were sunk deep in the sorrow of parting, helpless to understand or resist their tragic destinies. Leaning one against the other, they sank back onto the mat, as if lying down before the implacable advance of fate.

WU DAWANG RETURNED TO HIS home in western Henan, on leave.

A month and a half of furlough dragged like years in prison. He had no idea what had happened to Liu Lian after the Division Commander's return, or what discussions had taken place between his Captain and Political Instructor, or between his comrades-in-arms, when they got back from camp and field training to find him missing. His escape had gone entirely according to Liu Lian's meticulous plan. At ten o'clock on the morning of his departure, he arrived at the railway station where an official who specialized in arranging long-distance berths for high-ranking officers was waiting for him. After thrusting a ticket for a standard berth—a scarce commodity in those days—into his hand, the official showed him his special military travel permit. He then put the permit into an envelope and handed it to Wu

Dawang, instructing him to keep it safely on his person at all times—even when visiting the toilet.

His mission complete, the tall, thin officer returned to his office, leaving Wu Dawang standing alone in the large waiting room. And it was from this point on, in fact, that he was engulfed by a sense of solitude that descended on him as abruptly as, two months earlier, love had.

For the sake of appearances, Liu Lian didn't go with him to the station. In fact, she didn't even make it as far as the gate to Compound Number One, where the jeep that Management had sent was waiting for him. As they were about to say good-bye, the jeep sounded its horn. 'Take this,' she said, stuffing twenty crisp ten-*yuan* notes into his hand, 'and buy your wife some decent clothes, and your son some toys and treats.' He shook his head but she insisted, slipping the money into the leather briefcase she'd found for his travel documents.

The jeep honked its horn another couple of times.

As the tears rolled down his cheeks, she offered him a slight, gloomy smile. 'Liu Lian,' he said, taking her hand, 'will I ever see you again?'

After allowing him to clasp it for a minute, she withdrew her hand again. 'Off you go, the driver's waiting.' He had no choice but to turn and leave.

Though he'd hoped she would see him all the way to the jeep, he told her not to, and nor did she. As he drove away from the compound, however, he saw her emerge from the house. She stopped under the vine trellis and waved at the vehicle as it sped off, a brave, sad smile on her face.

He didn't know that the image of this last smile would dominate his memories of her for the rest of his life. And, during the painfully slow, lonely six weeks' leave that he endured in the Balou Mountains, that same smile was his main source of consolation.

Nor did he know that, during those same six weeks, the illustrious Division he had served in for the last five years was preparing—under pressure from invisible forces within—to vanish from the state military system. He didn't understand, either, how devastating the demobilization would be for so many people, or how many destinies his affair with Liu Lian was—directly or indirectly—to change. While it would be an exaggeration to claim that their liaison alone had destroyed an entire Division, without it fate would have dealt a very different hand to his comrades-in-arms. Little did Wu Dawang know—as he fretted away his leave—that his Division Commanders were conducting an elaborately premeditated, officially authorized operation to obliterate from view the Sergeant of the Catering Squad and his personal history.

Amnesia would become the Division's new watchword.

While the Division—as it set about its disappearing act—concentrated on forgetting him, Wu Dawang thought obsessively about the barracks, just as the life of a dying man flashes before his eyes, and grew easily impatient with the tedious pace of village life. And every night, once dusk had fallen, he found himself unable to resume normal marital relations with his wife.

Zhao Ezi was still his wife. Admittedly, she'd only ever demonstrated a kind of dull ineptitude in matters conjugal—an ability to speak out on inappropriate subjects at inappropriate moments that had utterly alienated the two of them from each

other. Her emotional idiocy had from the outset
blighted their attempts at intimacy. But nevertheless, ever since he had promised her a home in the
city, she had resolved to engage diligently in noc-
turnal manoeuvres with him. Though she continued to be embarrassed by sex and would never
make any unsolicited declaration of love, or ask him
to give her physical pleasure, she would for the
most part passively fall in with his own urges and
allow him free run of her whenever the mood took
him. Since becoming a Sergeant and a Party member especially, he had only to tell her about his lat-
est commendation, about the step closer toward
officialdom it had brought him, and she would smile
dutifully and let him proceed as he pleased, turning herself into a reward for successes so far
achieved, a motivation to carry him through the
struggles that remained.

In the few years that they had been married, she
and Wu Dawang had spent no more than two or
three months actually living together — not much
more than he'd spent with Liu Lian. But, in every
other way, these two periods of time were as different as Heaven and earth. While his wife viewed sex

as a prize for good behaviour, as the regrettable but necessary release of a primal instinct, Liu Lian saw it as an equal, creative exchange of pleasure.

Now, however, the happiness he had shared with Liu Lian lay entirely in the past. It existed only as a memory.

Probably because he was so busy remembering, for weeks following his return from the army, Wu Dawang did not make the slightest move in the direction of his wife. She was still the same simple, unaffected woman she had always been. Though she was nothing to look at compared to Liu Lian, though she lacked her sophistication, she did have certain qualities her rival lacked—youth being one. And as for the idea of sending him off to work in the kitchen—in her eyes, for him to cook her a meal would be an unthinkable humiliation. And she would never have let him wash dishes or clothes. If the neighbours saw him doing anything of that kind, they would think her positively debauched.

But working the land was his responsibility alone, and in this—taking in the corn, binding up the sheaves, ploughing, sowing the wheat, hauling dung, spreading fertilizer and so on—he was never less than diligent. But while farming kept him busy during the days, the nights offered no distraction.

The village of Wujiagou was made up of some twenty holdings dotted across a flank of the Balou Mountains, its hundred-odd inhabitants living off a combination of collective and private farming. On the wasted edges of a collectively owned field, for example, a villager might plant a few beans or sesame for his own family, or he might requisition a sandy bend of a river in which to sow cabbages and radishes. This was done not in the expectation that they would all grow to maturity and yield a full harvest, merely in the hope that whatever survived would help the family to scrape together their three daily meals. Every day Wu Dawang worked away in the fields, recounting to his fellow villagers what he had seen of the outside world. Every evening he would stay up long after his wife and son had gone to bed. Sitting in the courtyard by the house, or out on a nearby hillside, he would stare silently off in the direction in which his barracks lay, as if he were drunk, or deranged.

Perhaps a month after his return, in the middle of one of these nights, his wife nudged him with her elbow as he lay sleeping in bed. 'What's wrong?' she asked.

He pretended not to understand. 'What do you mean?'

'Is it because you haven't won any new commendations for the past six months? Is that why you won't touch me? You can have me if you want, as long as you keep working hard when you get back.'

This offer of sex on credit was the first encouragement she had given him, the first time she had intimated any form of physical desire. But he saw immediately that, as before, she continued to bind sex inextricably together with promotion — that she saw his desire for intimacy as a means for bettering her material situation, no different in essence from the hoe or pickax he used to turn the earth. As all this came back to him, his affection for her — such as it had been — withered into insignificance.

He refused either to touch her, or offer her reassurance. 'I swore an oath that if I failed to become an official, I'd never come near you again,' he told her almost primly as he sat up in bed. 'But I never thought it would take this long.' Hiding behind this pretext of bad conscience, he got out of bed and stood in the courtyard for a while, gazing up at the night sky. Somehow, the full moon brought forth such a frenzy of impossible, presumptuous thoughts about Liu Lian that, to calm himself, he walked off into the night, up a hill beyond the village. And there he stayed until dawn, when his wife appeared, calling out his name.

'It's almost morning,' she said, 'come back to bed.' At last he tried to explain himself to her, in sentiments worthy of the most exemplary socialist realist hero.

'I miss the barracks,' he sighed. 'Home's no fun, compared to the army.' And with that he turned and followed her back home.

After a month in Wujiagou—almost no time at all—Wu Dawang felt permanently on edge, as if his home were no longer home but a place of unbearable foreign exile. Whenever his eyes fell on the portrait of Chairman Mao hanging on the wall in his house, his expression would become distant, distracted, for reasons no one around him could have guessed. When he saw a plaster statue of the Chairman devoutly displayed on a neighbour's table, he would run his hand lovingly over it. If he passed a pupil from the village school carrying a copy of *The Quotations of Chairman Mao*, he would stop the child, flick aimlessly through the pages, then, equally aimlessly, hand it back. When, in the distance, he spotted the postman from town approaching the village, he would go out into the road to wait for him.

'Anything for me?' he would bellow, while the postman was still a way off.

'No,' the reply would drift back.

'No telegram?'

'If a telegram comes for you,' the postman would say, as he drew closer, 'you'll get it the night it arrives.'

One day, as he watched the postman cycling back into the distance, Wu Dawang impulsively sprinted after him, pulling so hard on his back pannier that the whole bike almost toppled over.

'Sure there's nothing for me?'

'What's wrong with you? You sick or something?' the man shouted back at him. 'Go back to the army and see a doctor!'

Wu Dawang stood at the edge of the village, staring at the departing postman like a man in love, unable to take his eyes off him until the blue post office bicycle faded into a pale dot, then disappeared in the late autumn sunlight.

In the end he withdrew almost entirely into himself. Unless his daily round of chores obliged him to do otherwise, he would not address a single word to either his wife or son.

The whole overheated situation came to a head after he discovered, as he was mucking out the pig-pen in the yard, a battered, wooden sign with 'Serve the People!' inscribed across it in black ink. Though the text was neither attributed to Mao Zedong nor illustrated with stars, ears of wheat or rifles, Wu Dawang placed the sign on the filthy wall of the pig-pen and glanced at it every time he threw out a shovel of dung. When he was ready to haul the dung out to the fields, he hung the sign on the carrying pole that he placed across his shoulders. As he ploughed and sowed, he left the sign at the edge of the field. When he took his son out to play, he would rest it on a branch.

One day, when his son accidentally trod on the sign after it had fallen from its branch. Wu Dawang slapped him so hard that bright red welts immediately sprang up on the little boy's face. Neither his wife nor his fellow villagers now felt they could responsibly stand by and allow matters to continue in this way. And so Wu Dawang's wife went looking for the leader of the village's production team and poured out some of the more perplexing details of their married life. In the first month Wu Dawang had been back, she related, he had not touched her once. But since he'd got hold of that sign, every night he would place it at the head of the bed, and every night he would want it. And when they did it, he treated her like—like an animal.

The team leader decided to pay Wu Dawang a visit that very day.

'Why are you still at home?' he asked first. 'Army leave is never more than a month, and you've been back almost six weeks now. Have they thrown you out for doing something wrong? If you've not been discharged, go back as soon as you can. If you're ill, get treated for it there. No one here can afford doctors or medicine, and you can't carry on like this. It's bad for you, and it's bad for your family.'

This conversation took place in the courtyard of Wu Dawang's thatched house. When the team leader arrived, Wu Dawang had been about to start building an energy-saving stove to reduce the family's fuel costs, making use of some of the skills he had learnt in the army. Because he needed silt from the courtyard, he had perched the Serve the People! sign on a pile of yellow earth. As he got up to leave, in order to emphasize his views about a certain other private matter, Wu Dawang's visitor glanced at the sign, then sent it flying with a single, well-aimed kick. Bits of rotten wood scattered over the courtyard like falling leaves, as the text disintegrated into unintelligible fragments.

The next day Zhao Ezi's father bustled over to the village. Because the venerable accountant was now so old that he himself had no further prospect of advancement, because he had toiled his whole life away in the commune without getting any of his sons or daughters moved to the city, the lines of angry frustration had sunk deep into his broad, weather-beaten face. On reaching Wu Dawang's house, he refused either to drink the water his daughter poured for him or to sit down on the stool that his son-in-law offered him, choosing instead to deliver his judgement standing up.

'I made the biggest mistake of my life when I let my daughter marry you.'

He drew Wu Dawang's neatly folded prenuptial agreement from an envelope, opened it out, batted furiously at the signature with his hand, flung it at his son-in-law and then stalked off back to the commune to complete the canteen's end-of-month accounts.

The document fluttered to the sandy ground, the sallow white of the paper almost exactly matching the colour of Wu Dawang's face.

The next day, he strapped his luggage together and returned to barracks.

XII

BY TRAIN, BUS AND EVEN juddering tractor, Wu
Dawang travelled the two days and one night back
to his Division. He was hardly tired by his long
journey—all that mattered was that soon he would
be back in barracks, and with this knowledge his
heart seemed to beat faster the closer he got. His face
was sweating with excited anxiety—as if he were a
felon returning to turn himself in to the authorities.

On the final leg of his journey, as he walked up to
the barracks, the plump autumn sun shone golden
light through the trees lining the road, through the
leaves that were starting to fall. It was so bright that
he needed to squint whenever he glanced upward.

Though the sentry on duty at the main gate did not
know him personally, it was obvious from his luggage
that Wu Dawang was just back from home leave.
Standing to attention, he saluted Wu Dawang and
called out a cheery 'Afternoon!' A little nonplussed

by this semiformal, semicasual greeting, Wu Dawang nodded back at him and raised his arms slightly, to explain his failure to return the salute.

'Sorry,' he said, 'too many bags.'

'No matter, no matter,' the sentry replied, smiling at him. 'Just back from leave?'

'That's right,' Wu Dawang answered.

'Why d'you bother coming back? Your company would have sent your things on to you.'

He stared uncomprehendingly at the sentry, as if puzzling at an insoluble equation. Noticing his bafflement, the sentry flashed Wu Dawang a cryptic smile. 'So you've not heard? Ah well—ignorance is bliss.'

'Heard what?' he asked, still staring and increasingly perplexed.

'Go back to barracks. You'll find out soon enough.'

'What on earth's happened?'

'You'll find out.'

Wu Dawang walked on.

It was usual practice for orderlies, when they returned from home leave, to report first to the house of the senior commanding officer they served. Only when the gifts brought back for him and his family had been handed over and all good wishes conveyed and received was an orderly allowed to go back to his company. But this time, for obvious reasons, Wu Dawang broke with custom and walked, a little shakily, straight past Compound Number One, casting only the briefest of glances in its direction.

The sight of the sparrows roosting peacefully on the windowsill of the first-floor bedroom told him that the window was not about to be thrown open. Perhaps Liu Lian was somewhere else. In any case, she couldn't have any idea that he was back. Before he'd left she'd warned him repeatedly not to return without a summons from his company.

But now, his nerve broken, he'd disregarded that warning.

As he approached his company barracks, a truck from a neighbouring company drove past him, lined with soldiers in full uniform and packed with their rucksacks. Each face had the same grim set to it, as if they were on their way to carry out a distasteful, but unavoidable mission. On the side of the truck closest to Wu Dawang hung a banner made of red cloth, emblazoned with the slogan: 'Wherever I Wander is My Home'.

The truck hadn't been going much faster than walking pace, but when it reached Wu Dawang's company barracks, the driver changed gears and accelerated to cycling speed. At that moment two bottles of liquor suddenly flew out and smashed against the red-brick gable of the company office. A volley of profanities followed the bottles and the truck drove off.

A moment later, almost as if he'd been expecting just such an incident, the company's Signals Officer scurried out with a dustpan and brush and deftly swept up the fragments of glass.

Wu Dawang called out to him.

Although the officer turned to glance at him, he walked back into the building as if he hadn't heard a thing, leaving Wu Dawang even more confused. As he stood there, desperately trying to make sense of things, his Political Instructor appeared in the main doorway and strode over to greet Wu Dawang.

'Sergeant,' he began, as he approached, 'weren't you told to stay at home until we recalled you?' He hurried Wu Dawang inside, told him to sit down and poured him some hot water to drink. He then ran some tap water so Wu Dawang could wash his face, and even brought out his precious made-in-Shanghai scented soap so that his visitor could wash the dust of the journey off his hands. This sequence of extraordinarily hospitable acts went some way to calming Wu Dawang's jangled nerves. The Political Instructor next asked Wu Dawang how his journey had been and, on discovering that the returning Sergeant had not had lunch, immediately told the Signals Officer to ask the canteen to stir-fry him a bowl of egg noodles.

While Wu Dawang ate, the Political Instructor informed him of the following.

First, that the Division Commander's wife had personally told them that because of serious family problems Wu Dawang required a three-month period of home leave, and an extended furlough had accordingly been granted. As long as there was no urgent business calling him back to barracks, he could take as long as he needed.

Secondly, that at a seminar in Beijing organized and directed by the Central Military Commission, the Division Commander had volunteered for an assignment that no other Division had been prepared to take on: to test out a pilot scheme aimed at streamlining and restructuring the entire army. In practical terms, this meant that the Division was to be disbanded; that, within the vast machinery of the People's Liberation Army, it was to disappear like so much smoke.

Thirdly, given that the majority of companies were to be demobilized and a minority transferred, all promotions had, for the time being, been cancelled. This meant that Wu Dawang's dream of becoming an official looked doomed, yet again, to founder — this time on the rocks of bureaucratic mischance. But because he was such a favourite of the Division Commander and his wife, the former had left instructions that an exception was to be made in his case. A job was to be arranged for Wu Dawang in a city in his native province. His family were to be moved there also, and appropriate work found for his wife.

' Fourthly, with all the restructuring going on, the personnel situation in barracks was currently extremely unstable. As a result, there had been a high turnover of staff in the Division Commander's household. Though each orderly had taken pains to conduct himself with cautious discretion inside Compound Number One, and though Liu Lian had done her best to smooth things over, each had somehow succeeded in provoking the Commander's wrath. Because of the present uncertainty of the Commander's temper, it was requested that Wu Dawang should not return to his old post; indeed, that he should not visit the house at all, unless some matter of pressing importance called him there.

As he listened to the Political Instructor, a feeling of enormous relief flooded through Wu Dawang. The anxiety that had overtaken him as soon as he had reached the Division barracks began to ease: his affair with Liu Lian remained undiscovered.

Mass demobilization and Wu Dawang's own imminent departure seemed to be bringing this unusual tale of romance to a brusque close; fate had assertively ruled against the happy reunion of our lovers. The Political Instructor offered a kind of consolation prize—to sweeten the bitterness of separation— granting Wu Duwang a brief period of calm before unhappiness reclaimed him.

His company's Captain was nowhere to be seen. Earlier in his career he himself had once served as the Division Commander's Orderly (at exactly the time, in fact, when the Commander had reluctantly parted company with his first wife). The Captain therefore enjoyed much closer relations with Liu Lian and her husband than the Political Instructor did. It was this intimacy that made Wu Dawang keen to learn more from him about what was going on—he was like a murderer torn between wanting to keep up the appearance of innocence and to find out if anyone knew about his crime. So, once the afternoon study session was underway, he told the Political Instructor he had an urgent report to make to the Captain. After considering this request, the Instructor asked the Signals Officer to help him find the Captain—even though he himself would have known perfectly well where he was and what he was doing.

The Signals Officer led Wu Dawang to the southernmost end of the barracks, to the rooms of the Commander of the Third Battalion, Second Regiment. The battalion barracks were fronted by a large copse of tung trees, whose withered, yellow leaves had formed a gloomily autumnal carpet over the ground. A sentry stood in the doorway to the Battalion Commander's quarters—short, stout and stubbornly conscientious to the point of refusing them entry. The Commander, he informed them, had been most particular that no one should be allowed in. So they waited by the door while he disappeared inside to report their arrival, and see if the Captain of the Guards Company was available.

He kept them waiting for what felt like an inordinate length of time. Fidgety with impatience, Wu Dawang took himself over to the Battalion Commander's window. Through it he witnessed a scene that gave him his first, glimmering sense that perhaps his entanglement with Liu Lian had not been as straightforwardly personal an affair as he thought. He could see the Commander's desk piled with dishes, bowls and empty bottles of the local sorghum-distilled liquor. A dozen or so scarlet chopsticks lay scattered on the floor.

The Commander and his four guests had obviously been drinking since lunchtime, for at least three of them now looked too far gone for any more sense to be got out of them that day. As a stunned Wu Dawang took in this debauched display, he noted that, in addition to the Battalion Commander and Wu Dawang's own Captain, the party included the Deputy Commander of the Third Regiment, the Political Instructor of the Third Battalion and a staff officer from Division HQ. These individuals neither shared a common place of origin nor had they fought alongside each other. The one thing that united them was their link to the Division Commander — they had all served him either as Personal Orderly, Bodyguard or Signals Officer earlier in his career, when he was only a Captain or Battalion Commander.

Nevertheless, Wu Dawang couldn't fathom why they should have gathered in this dissolute, undisciplined manner, tarnishing the dignity of their military office. The Deputy Commander was prostrate, snoring, on the bed. The Staff Officer was on the floor, leaning against the bed, crying hysterically. Or perhaps he was laughing: it was hard to tell from the other side of the window. Their host, in the meantime, had squatted down by the legs of the table and was slapping his own face, muttering over and over, 'Why couldn't you keep your damned mouth shut?' The Captain and Political Instructor, by contrast, still seemed to be relatively *compos mentis*, as they attempted to reason with the Battalion Commander. 'It's too soon to worry,' they appeared to be saying, 'we don't yet know who's being demobilized, and who's being transferred.'

But the Battalion Commander simply sat there, roaring with mirthless laughter. 'I know what's going to happen! I know!'

At this instant, the Captain happened to turn round and spot Wu Dawang looking in at them all. Paling, he glanced at his fallen comrades, then abandoned the Battalion Commander and strode out of the room to confront their eavesdropper. 'What are you doing back here again?' he barked at him, yanking him away from the window.

'I'd been at home over a month, Captain.'

'Have you been to the Division Commander's house?'

'Not yet.'

Heaving a sigh of relief, the Captain went back inside to say something, then came out again to drag Wu Dawang and the Signals Officer back to barracks. On the way, he issued a single command to his Sergeant. 'Tell no one anything you heard or saw just now. If any—any of this—reaches the Division Commander, we're all of us finished.' After that, he was silent.

And so Wu Dawang returned to barracks, still unable to make sense of a single thing going on around him. He didn't really trouble himself with the complexities of the restructuring. He thought only of his affair with Liu Lian, and of the succulent fruits of victory that it was going to bring him: honourable discharge from the army, and jobs for him and his wife in the city.

To begin with, this was exactly how simple everything appeared to Wu Dawang. In the short time that he'd been back in the army, he'd been genuinely taken aback by how happily things were working out for him. It looked as if his untimely reappearance in barracks had made the Division authorities desperate to be rid of him again, and as quickly as possible. Within a week he and his family had been fixed up with work and housing in the city nearest their village. While his comrades-in-arms agonized over the uncertainty of their prospects, all Wu Dawang had to do to assure his own future was fill in and sign a few forms handed to him by army bureaucrats. That was all.

Wu Dawang's army career drew to a close so fast that it almost took him by surprise. For his last few days, he tried to put thoughts of the restructuring — of its Strengthening of the National Economy and Improving of the People's Livelihood — to one side.

Instead, he took the opportunity to wander about, reacquainting himself with the barracks after his long absence, calling on comrades-in-arms from his village, washing his bedding and clothes. At night, he struggled to temper his impossible longing for Liu Lian by sternly reminding himself how fortunate he'd been to enjoy the time he'd had with her.

But this exceptional period of idleness also gave Wu Dawang time to reflect on everything that had gone before, hardening his suspicions that the entire course of this affair of his had formed part of an elaborately choreographed scheme. He was beginning to sense that his liaison with Liu Lian was a piece of theatre scripted and directed from behind the scenes, in which his only freedom had been whether or not to engage emotionally with the role he had been cast in. As his suspicions grew, he could feel the intensity of his feelings waning, but he was still unwilling to acknowledge the absence of any real emotional honesty in his relationship with Liu Lian. Nor could he replace his fairytale memories of their affair with hardheaded contemplation of how it might relate to the way the Division was being dismantled. He refused to believe that the Division

Commander would, for purely self-interested reasons, exploit the Central Party Streamlining Initiative in order to scatter his own troops like autumn leaves. Even though three battalions and four companies had already been banished to a remote frontier division five hundred miles away, still Wu Dawang would not believe it. Over the past two days, however, the Corps Commander—the Division Commander's immediate superior—had arrived to take charge of the restructuring and demobilization. This was clearly a serious business. Wu Dawang had witnessed how troops, on the eve of their departure, would sit woodenly through their farewell banquets. Then afterward, emboldened by liquor, they would seek out isolated corners of the barracks on which to vent their anger, shattering windows and smashing equipment that had been with them through years of struggle, honour and disgrace. In the minutes before leaving, they would weep openly in front of each other, resigned never to meet again in this life.

But still they left: the First Regiment in its entirety, then the First Battalion of the Second Regiment, then the Machine Gunners.

The previous afternoon, Wu Dawang had taken himself quietly over to the Machine Gunners' barracks, by which point the entire company—which had twice won collective commendations in the Civil War—had already been dispatched in five trucks marked 'Liberation' to the special military-transport station. Chaos—as complete as the chaos he and Liu Lian had spread throughout the Division Commander's house some two months ago—prevailed in the empty building.

But while the disorder that he and Liu Lian had generated had been an expression of their love for each other, the cheerless anarchy of the Machine Gunners' barracks spoke only of despair and uncertainty. Wooden guns used in drill practice lay uselessly on the floors, while the rubber coating on a vaulting horse had been hacked into scars that gaped like screaming mouths. Across the notice board that in happier days had been the mouthpiece of discipline and orthodoxy, someone had scrawled 'Fuck you all'.

On the paper strips used to seal off the vacated dormitories, someone else had scribbled a few lines of mournfully ironic doggerel in red pen: 'Our

Helmsman guides us over the seas, sailing where the currents please; when the sea goes east so do we, as free as the wind and rain.'

Beneath a vermilion sunset, Wu Dawang stood at the main door to the deserted barracks, feeling the desolation wash over him. Though he knew that he owed the departing Machine Gunners a few tears, his eyes remained obstinately dry. It dawned on him that he was, deep down, indifferent to the distress his comrades felt as they were restructured back to the dead-end homes from which they'd come. The true source of his pain was the warning he'd been given against returning to the Division Commander's house.

On his way back to barracks, he bumped into the Head of Management, who needed his signature on a job assignment form. Once the document had been signed, he patted Wu Dawang on the shoulder and flashed him a mysterious smile. 'Thanks to Liu Lian,' he remarked, 'you've come out of this better than any of us.' And off he went with his form, leaving Wu Dawang still pondering his words—and that ambiguous smirk of his—until past dinnertime.

After lights-out that evening, as the Division collectively closed its eyes and prepared for sleep, Wu Dawang lay wide awake, thinking things over. For some reason, in the daytime he was able to keep the restructuring separate in his mind from his affair with Liu Lian, but at night the one would always surreptitiously become intertwined with the other.

That particular evening, the suspicion that a trick had somehow been played on him was eating away at him. But when he thought back to his time with Liu Lian and to the many ways she'd been good to him, his memories of her marvellous body and smooth, flawless skin soothed his sense of wounded pride like a balm. As he shifted restlessly in bed, recollection of those intense, exhilarating days revived hopeless, romantic dreams, destroying his hard-won peace of mind. For an irrational moment, all that he had achieved so far—his distinguished army career, his imminent painless return to civilian life, the transfer of his family to the city—together with the traumatic breaking up of the Division, paled into insignificance next to the euphoria he'd felt with Liu Lian. His longing to see her — just one more time — swept away everything in its path.

Late that night he plucked up courage. Creeping out of bed, he put his uniform back on and padded off in the direction of the Division Commander's house. But just as he was about to leave the barracks behind, a furious roar brought him to an instant halt.

'What the hell do you think you're doing?'

Turning around, Wu Dawang found his Captain standing only a few steps behind him. He couldn't be sure whether the Captain had been up and about anyway, or whether he'd been followed. Wu Dawang took refuge in the shadow of a tree, while the Captain stationed himself under a streetlamp, his face flushed with rage.

'Get back to barracks!' the Captain barked at him again, after a few minutes of this face-off. Wu Dawang obediently turned back toward his dormitory, past the Captain. As he drew level with his superior, the Captain spoke to him again, still reprimanding but in a gentler, more brotherly tone. 'You have to remember you're … the son of a peasant, while she — she's the Division Commander's wife. It's not as if you've been punished for what you did.

The Commander's even fixed you and your family up with jobs in the city. What have you got to complain about?'

Wu Dawang paused.

'Go back to bed,' the Captain went on. 'No one but me has guessed.'

Still Wu Dawang remained where he was, staring at his Captain.

'I was his Orderly before he became Division Commander, remember. D'you think I don't know why his first wife divorced him for a factory worker? Come on, Sergeant, have a sense of proportion: in three days' time, they're going to tell everyone left in barracks who's going to be demobilized and who's going to be transferred. While everyone else is going out of their minds with worry, here you are, moping about in your own fantasy world. Take a long hard look at yourself: is this the stuff a revolutionary soldier is made of? The way you are now, I have no idea why the Division Commander thought enough of you to make you his Orderly. And I can't understand what Liu Lian saw in you either.'

Wu Dawang thought back to the scene he'd stumbled upon three days ago in the Battalion

Commander's room—to those five drunk, despairing officers, all former staff in the Division Commander's household. 'Will our company be demobilized, too?'

'Maybe it will and maybe it won't,' the Captain replied. 'But one thing's certain—you're not going to help matters by calling on Liu Lian.'

Bowing his head, Wu Dawang made his way back in silence.

From then on he confined himself to his dormitory, sleeping away his few remaining days in barracks. And, just as the Captain had said, three days later at noon, Wu Dawang received formal notification of his demobilization. Shortly afterward his immediate superiors called him in.

'Time to celebrate, I think,' the Political Instructor told him. 'Guess where you've been assigned a job—the biggest factory in the city, The East is Red Tractor Factory. The manager there ranks higher than a Provincial Governor, or a Corps Commander.'

'Don't waste money celebrating with us,' the Captain cautioned. 'Life is expensive in the city, so save what you can now. Off you go and pack. You're due to report to the factory the day after tomorrow, which means you'll need to catch a train today to get settled in before your first day at work.'

After this conversation—in truth, no more than a terse, one-way dispatch outlining the logistics of Wu Dawang's expulsion from barracks—the two officers helped him truss up his luggage.

Every last detail had been taken care of—urgently and meticulously, and far, far above Wu Dawang's head. The moment the details of his departure had been settled the Division even sent over a plentiful supply of cardboard boxes and wooden crates for his belongings and rope to secure them. Despite this note of almost unseemly haste, everything proceeded in a perfectly smooth, disciplined fashion. As Wu Dawang's train wasn't due to leave until 12:30 that night, his company laid on a lavish last supper for him, with a farewell meeting to follow.

After dinner the hundred-strong company—all in full uniform—stayed on in the mess, perched on small stools. Once a few songs had been sung and a few quotations by Chairman Mao recited, the Political Instructor announced that Wu Dawang was receiving a special early discharge to take up a factory job in the city. The news was greeted with silent astonishment by the assembled company. Immediately afterward, the Head of Management—who, unusually, had come along to bid Wu Dawang farewell in person—gave public notice that the departing Sergeant was being honoured with the Third Order of Merit.

Through diligent study of *The Collected Works of Chairman Mao*, he read out, Wu Dawang had become an outstanding revolutionary thinker of excellent moral character. Thanks to his overwhelming success in putting theory into practice, he'd been awarded the unique accolade of Exemplary Servant of the People—the only soldier in the whole Division to be thus feted. Why, he asked rhetorically, was Wu Dawang being honoured with a state-allocated job? Because he Served the People with all his body and soul. It should be pointed out that none of them—not Wu Dawang, his Captain or his Political Instructor—had known in advance that the evening's performance would end like this.

Finally, the Head of Management and the Political Instructor jointly exhorted the assembled company to learn from Comrade Wu Dawang's example, reminding their audience that the People only remembered and helped those who selflessly Served them. If they all gave something of themselves, as Wu Dawang had, the army would help them, just as they had helped Wu Dawang find a job that would enable him to continue making the utmost contribution to socialism.

Wu Dawang said nothing. Even when he got up to receive his badge of merit and the Political Instructor repeatedly asked him to address a few words to his audience, he merely bowed impassively to his comrades-in-arms, then turned to salute the ranking officers standing alongside him on the stage.

Formal festivities came to an end.

Back at the dormitory, he found his Captain sticking railway labels on the last of his luggage. He flashed Wu Dawang a bitter smile: 'I'll be off soon myself,' he said. 'I've just had notice of my own demobilization. Everyone who worked in the Division Commander's house is leaving. We've only ourselves to blame: we said what we shouldn't have said. Or at least, someone said too much about the Commander and his wives, though I don't know how it got back to him.'

'So that's what's behind it all?'

Another smile. 'Maybe it is and maybe it isn't. I'm just guessing.'

Wu Dawang and the Captain stood facing each other, in silence, for some time.

As Wu Dawang's departure approached, a crescent moon rose in the sky and hooked itself precariously over a cloud. When the Management jeep pulled up to drive him to the station, his entire company came out to see him off: to shake his hand, to offer their congratulations, to wish him well. 'As long as they keep us on in the army,' everyone seemed to want to say to him, 'we'll all try and learn to Serve the People like you.' Wu Dawang had nothing to say to this; he merely shook hands and bid his farewells, until he'd taken leave of one and all and it was time to get into the jeep. He had been determined not to cry, but when the engine fired up his emotions finally got the better of him. As his last journey out of barracks began, the tears rolled down his cheeks.

ALL WAS DRAWING TO A satisfactory conclusion.

Standing by the jeep were Wu Dawang's Captain, his Political Instructor and the Head of Management, who remarked gloomily that now they'd seen Wu Dawang off it would soon be his own turn. He was not yet forty, he said, and would have accepted a demotion happily enough if that would have kept him in the army, but he'd just heard he might be demobilized instead. He had to go and see the Division Commander and beg him to let him stay on. He paused, then smiled wryly at his two fellow officers. 'It's every man for himself now. Finish the job off for me, will you? Make sure Wu Dawang gets to the station.'

Once the Head of Management had watched the car drive away, he walked straight over to Division HQ. The jeep raced away, its headlamps coursing through the darkness. The moon had risen higher, illuminating the newly bare autumn trees into bleak silhouettes. No nightingales or cicadas disturbed the still night with their chirruping song. By now, lights-out had sounded and each company, hoping that a final display of perfect obedience might win them a last-minute reprieve, had dutifully fallen into a troubled sleep. The vast majority was blissfully unaware that within their very own barracks the final curtain was falling on an unlikely romance. Only the key protagonists and a few of the minor players in our story had any inkling that this microdrama was nearing its end. And, of these, none anticipated the desolate postscript to the affair that would sour the grand finale the army bureaucracy had choreographed.

The jeep sped by first one row of army buildings, then another, past trees and pylons that fell behind it as if felled by the dazzling, bladelike beams of its lights. Wu Dawang sat alone on one side, with the Captain and Political Instructor opposite him, making fussy small talk — had he checked his tickets, there was no time to spare, checking luggage in always took forever — before falling silent. All three men sank so deeply into private, melancholy thought that as the jeep passed by the senior officers' compound, not one of them so much as glanced in its direction. But just as the jeep was about to leave the barracks, out of the corner of his eye Wu Dawang saw a first-floor light come on in Compound Number One — in Liu Lian's bedroom. It seemed to set something inside him alight, too, flooding his ashen face with colour. He looked back once, twice, at the light. Then, before it was too late, he shouted at the driver to stop.

He braked hard. 'What is it?'

Ignoring him, Wu Dawang rummaged for something out of one of his bags, then jumped out of the vehicle and set off toward the house.

'Stop right there!' the Captain bellowed at him.

He did not stop, but he did slow down.

'If you go up to that house,' the Captain went on, at the same volume, 'you'll pay for it. You're not out of the army yet — your personal dossier's not going out until tomorrow.'

Wu Dawang halted.

The Political Instructor, however, smiled patiently at the Captain. 'The Division Commander's still in the office,' he soothed. 'Let him go and say good-bye, it's fair enough.'

The Captain fell silent. The Political Instructor leapt down from the jeep and accompanied Wu Dawang on his last walk to the Division Commander's house.

The two hundred metres between the main gate and the Commanders' Compound were far better lit than the rest of the road. Wu Dawang was still flushed, perhaps after his Captain's furious rebuke or in remembrance of the strange, compromised kind of love Liu Lian had offered him. As the two of them advanced, shoulder to shoulder, the Instructor delivered in a hushed voice a final philosophical lecture of a rather different kind from his usual offerings. 'In all the meetings and classes we've had together, I've told you nothing but lies and empty words. Now you're leaving, I might as well tell you the truth. At the end of the day, we're all here on earth to make our lives a bit better. A soldier born to a worker dreams of becoming an official; a soldier born to a low-ranking official dreams of becoming a high-ranking official; a soldier from the countryside wants to make it to the city. It might not be what we're meant to dream of, but that's how it is. And though climbing up one rung of the ladder might not sound much as an ambition, it ends up taking most people a lifetime. We both know the Division's going to the wall—almost everyone's going to be sent home. Which means almost everyone in barracks will lose any hope of realizing their dream. Whereas you—in less than three days you've achieved everything you ever hoped for. Remember that when you see Liu Lian this last time—keep yourself in check and make a good final impression. After all, you never know when you might need her to help you out of a tight spot in the future. Hey—are you listening to me?'

'Yes,' Wu Dawang finally replied. 'You've no need to worry, Sir.'

They arrived.

After exchanging salutes with the sentry, they reached the entrance to Number One. The rules about lights-out were not as strict for the Commanders as for everyone else, and the Compound's six residences blazed with light while the barracks were sunk in darkness. The sound of singing drifted out from a radio into the night. Through the familiar iron gate, Wu Dawang could see the vine trellis. With only half its yellowed leaves still clinging to its twisted branches, the pale moonlight spilled through it onto the ground before the house like strips of torn white silk. The grapes had finished some weeks ago but a faint, sour-sweet scent of fruit still hung over the trellis. Wu Dawang inhaled deeply, as if wanting to hold the fragrance inside him. He was preparing to open the unlocked gate when the Political Instructor suddenly pulled him back. 'I need your help with something,' he said.

The moon shone bright enough for Wu Dawang to notice the embarrassment on the Instructor's face.

'Me, help you?'

'You're the only one who can.'

'I'll help if I possibly can.'

'I can see for myself that you have a special relationship with Liu Lian—you're more than an orderly to her. Just before you leave, could you ask her to speak to the Division Commander for me? You see, they told me today I'm going to be demobilized, and I need her to persuade the Commander to let me stay. In all my years in the Division, I haven't made a single mistake. I've been a model Political Instructor, I've won prizes for my work. I don't mind missing out on promotion, but I need to stay in the army another year or two—any company will do. By the end of next year I'll have been here fifteen years, which means my wife can join me whether I get promoted or not. I'll be completely straight with you: my father-in-law is the Head of Militia in his commune and he only let me marry his daughter because he thought if he sent me off to the army I'd be able to get her a job in the city. I had to write him a prenuptial guarantee, swearing that I'd do whatever it took. Help me out, Wu Dawang, get Liu Lian to talk to the Division Commander.'

Wu Dawang stared at him, too surprised by the similarity between the Instructor's marriage and his own to respond.

His superior smiled awkwardly. 'I know I shouldn't have asked, but it was my last chance before you left. You go in and do whatever seems right. If she's got company, forget it, but if she's on her own, try and put a word in for me.'

Wu Dawang glanced across at the flower beds and noted that the flowers—the chrysanthemums and peonies especially—needed pruning. Some plants wanted cutting back to their roots in autumn so that they could store up food for the winter and shoot up again in spring. Before he could share this basic piece of gardening know-how with the Political Instructor, so he could pass it on to the new Orderly, they reached the front door. The Political Instructor stepped forward and announced that he was Reporting for Duty.

'Who is it?' they both heard Liu Lian shout out from upstairs.

'The Political Instructor from the Guards.'

Her footsteps creaked softly down the stairs.

It was obvious that Liu Lian was alone in the house. Proving himself to be, after all, a man of tact and sensitivity, the Political Instructor pushed Wu Dawang forward, then retreated into his shadow.

The door opened and Liu Lian appeared dressed in a bright red, knitted nightgown, almost as heavy as a coat. Perhaps it hadn't even occurred to her that Wu Dawang might try to catch one more glimpse of her before leaving—her hair was dishevelled, her face sallow with fatigue. More importantly, beneath her robe her stomach protruded slightly, but distinctly. She was clearly pregnant. Suddenly aware of the apparent unseemliness of the situation, she glared at the Political Instructor, who gazed off into the middle distance, pretending not to notice. In awkward silence she and Wu Dawang stood facing each other across the threshold, each waiting for the other to speak. Wu Dawang was bewildered—mesmerized—by the bulge of her stomach, unable to take his eyes off it. At last, with a poke in the back from the Political Instructor, he managed a couple of words. 'I'm leaving,' he said softly.

'I know,' she replied. 'On the 12:30 train.'

'I wanted to see you, just one more time, before I went.' He held out a shiny paper bag to her, as if returning something she had lost and he had found.

She glanced down at his outstretched hand. 'What is it?'

'It's a packet of pine kernels. They're a present I brought you from home.' Finally accepting the bag, she examined it carefully, and even opened it and tried one. Still chewing, she turned and went upstairs without a word.

That crumpled bag of pine nuts broke the impasse of this last encounter. During her absence Wu Dawang took the opportunity to step inside. In the sitting room, all was exactly as it had been when he had first started work in the house, except that in place of the framed quotation exhorting its beholder to 'Take Pride in the Traditions of the Revolution, Struggle for Glory' that they had smashed, there now hung another, equally large glass-framed print declaring that 'Without a People's Army, the People Have Nothing'. He wanted to take a look in the kitchen as well—his centre of operations for so many months and the place where, in many respects, life had truly begun for him. And around the dining room, to see whether that all-important sign was still there. He wanted to ask Liu Lian if she would give it to him—as a souvenir.

But just as he thought he might explore further, Liu Lian came swiftly down the stairs, holding a rectangular object—half an inch thick, a few inches wide, just over a foot long—wrapped in red silk. She walked over and handed it silently to Wu Dawang.

'What's this?' he asked.

'What you were about to ask for.' He pulled the silk back at a corner. Blushing, he hastily wrapped it back up.

'Sister,' he murmured, looking across at her.

After glancing nervously out of the door, she raised her hand to stroke his face. 'Did your Political Instructor ask you to ask me to speak to the Division Commander for him?'

Wu Dawang nodded.

The rims of Liu Lian's eyes seemed to redden. 'I'm afraid you'll have to tell him and your Captain that I'm sorry, I can't help them. The authorities have already approved the Commander's final report and agreed that all troops remaining in barracks are to be sent home. You've all suffered because of me. Quick, off you go now and tell the Captain and the Instructor that I'll do whatever I can to help them after they've left the army.'

Wu Dawang stayed put.

'Off you go, the Division Commander's going to be home any minute.'

Still Wu Dawang did not move, his face pale, uncomprehending.

Her mouth twisting into a kind of smile, Liu Lian took his hand and ran it over her swelling stomach, then urged him again to go. 'Best hurry,' she shouted out at the Political Instructor, still standing in the shadows, 'or he'll miss his train.'

As she walked them to the gate Wu Dawang could smell the scent of sweet, ripe apple on her as it floated off into the night air.

Three days later, the final demobilization of the division was officially announced. All those who knew of Wu Dawang's affair with Liu Lian, and all those who did not, were scattered to the winds. The secret sank without trace, like a piece of gold thrown into the sea.

EPILOGUE

WU DAWANG ENTERED MIDDLE AGE. While the details of his life over the previous decade and a half—how exactly he, his wife and son had enjoyed their heavenly urban existence—would have eluded a casual observer, the physical toll the years had taken was readily apparent in the resigned creases of his expression, in the coarsening of his complexion. A closer look might have caught, in addition to the lines time had etched, a mood of melancholy that aged him far beyond his years. His was a face that had admitted failure, its strength sapped by the social transformations that had bewildered and exhausted his generation. Even in his youth, he had shown little defiant swagger when confronted by life's tribulations. And now, fifteen years after his departure from the army, as he reappeared at the gate to the Commanders' Compound in the military quarter of the provincial capital, any fighting spirit had been truly ground out of him. He had known for some time that his old Division Commander had been made Provincial Commander-in-Chief, while his beautiful wife Liu Lian continued to bask in her husband's reflected glory. A quick glance at the television or newspaper told him all he needed to know about the former Division Commander's situation in life, but his only clues about Liu Lian were fragments of hearsay from former comrades-in-arms with an ear for society gossip.

One winter's day, as a thick blanket of snow settled over the buildings, ring road and overpasses of the provincial capital, Wu Dawang's eye was caught by a boy in his midteens from the Supreme Commanders' Compound in the military quarter, skating and sliding at dusk with a crowd of other children over the frozen Jinshui river. After studying him from a distance for some time, Wu Dawang, dressed in an old-fashioned army coat, set off down the wide road that ran east along the river. Soon he found himself at the main gate to the Commanders' Compound.

This gate bore no resemblance to its counterpart in the former Division barracks that lay a couple of hundred miles east of the provincial capital, and had long since become a sprawling factory complex. The gate in front of Wu Dawang had pretensions to the monumental, flanked on either side by pillars that towered like city walls, their great capitals clad, at unimaginable expense, in imported stone. The gate's crossbeam—clad in this same stone—was studded with ingeniously recessed electric lights and hung with two enormous lanterns left over from National Day celebrations. Two sentries were stationed on two square, red-and-white striped platforms half a foot off the ground. Each shouldered rifles, obliged by the aura of imposing immensity that attached itself to the gate and to the Compound, and by the constant audience of traffic and passersby, to stand guard in stiff, solemn silence. Wu Dawang did not approach the gate but kept his distance on the pavement outside, observing the Compound's comings and goings until past ten o'clock that night, when he disappeared into the bustling city.

He paid his second visit the following morning. His years in the army enabled him to make a few common sense deductions about how one might gain entry to such a compound. As a result he strolled, unchallenged, past the sentries and on toward Number One.

Though different in detail, the general pattern of the place was remarkably similar to the house and garden in which Wu Dawang had worked fifteen years ago. Behind wrought-iron railings lay a patchwork of flower beds and bare vegetable plots, their furrows still visible beneath the snow. There was even a trellis covered in wiry vines, its network of snow-coated branches like frosted fish scales. Into Number One's gate — which was large enough for cars to pass through — was set a smaller gate for pedestrians. As Wu Dawang approached, a sentry standing to one side of the weather-beaten gatepost stared suspiciously at him. After issuing him with a chilly good morning, the sentry asked, in a louder voice, who he was looking for.

'Liu Lian,' Wu Dawang replied. 'Fifteen years ago, when her husband was in charge of my Division, I was the Orderly in their house.'

'Do the Commander and his wife know you're coming?'

'How else would I have got through the main gate?'

Retreating into his sentry box, the soldier picked up the phone to ring the Commander's house. 'Tell Liu Lian that my name is Wu Dawang and that I'm waiting at the gate,' Wu Dawang added. After a short exchange, the sentry replaced the receiver and came back out. Looking Wu Dawang up and down a couple of times, he pushed open the iron gate and passed through the courtyard into the building, leaving Wu Dawang to wait outside. Because of the compound's size, its protective shield of trees and the soft, heavy falling of the snow, Wu Dawang felt enveloped by a curious sense of stillness, far from the commotion of the city. Under the gloomy, ashen sky—a whirling mass of snowflakes—his head and coat were quickly covered in a fine white down. Just as he was starting to feel the cold, the gaunt sentry re-emerged and passed him a sealed envelope. 'Aunt Liu's having her hair done so she can't invite you in,' he reported, 'but she said if there was anything you needed you should write it on the letter and she'll sort it out.'

Opening the envelope, a bewildered Wu Dawang found two terse lines:

If there's something you need my help with, say
what it is underneath. If it's money you want, write
the amount and the address to send it to.

From the gate Wu Dawang stared reproachfully
at the front door. As the snow continued to fly about
him, he folded up the letter, placed it back inside the
envelope, and felt inside his coat for a stiff rectangular object — half an inch thick, a few inches wide,
just over a foot long — wrapped in red silk, like a lim-
ited edition gift box of cigarettes. 'Just give this to
Liu Lian,' he said, handing it to the sentry.

And then he turned and walked away, vanishing
into the snow.

POSTSCRIPT

THIS SPEECH WAS DELIVERED BY Comrade Mao Zedong on 8 September 1944, at a meeting held by the departments reporting directly to the Central Committee of the Communist Party of China, to honour the memory of Comrade Zhang Side.

Our Communist Party, and the Eighth Route and New Fourth Armies led by our Party, are battalions of the revolution — totally devoted to the liberation of the people and working entirely in the interests of the people. Comrade Zhang Side served in the ranks of these battalions.

All men must die one day, but not all deaths have the same significance. The ancient Chinese writer Sima Qian said, 'Though it is certain all men must die, some deaths carry more weight than Mount Tai, while others carry less weight than a feather.' To die for the cause of the people carries more weight than Mount Tai, but to waste one's energy in the service of the fascists and to die for the exploiters and the oppressors carries less weight than a feather. Comrade Zhang Side died serving the interests of the people, and his death carries more weight than Mount Tai.

We serve the people and therefore, if we have shortcomings, we are not afraid to have them pointed out and criticized. Any individual, whoever it may be, can point out our shortcomings. If he is right, we will correct ourselves. If what he proposes is beneficial to the people, we will act upon it. The suggestion to have 'fewer but better troops and a simplified administration' was made by Mr. Li Dingming, who is not a Communist. This was a good idea, it was beneficial to the people, so we adopted it. If, in the interests of the people, we persevere in doing what is right and in correcting what is wrong, everyone in our ranks will thrive.

We hail from all corners of our country and have gathered here with one common revolutionary objective in mind. The vast majority of people need to come with us on the road to this objective. Today we already have operations bases covering areas with a population of ninety-one million people, but this is not enough; we need a greater network of bases if we are to liberate the whole nation. In difficult times our comrades must not lose sight of our successes, they must recognize our bright future, and must pluck up their courage. The Chinese people are suffering and it is our duty to save them; we will need to use all our might and main in this struggle. Now, when there is struggle there is sacrifice: death is a common occurrence. As we have taken to heart the interests of the people and the suffering of the great majority of the people, to die for the people is to give that death real significance. Nevertheless, we must keep unnecessary sacrifices to a minimum. Our officers must be mindful of every soldier, and every member of every revolutionary battalion must look after each other, and must love and help each other.

From now on, when anyone in our ranks dies, whether he be a cook or a soldier, if he has done anything useful at all, his funeral should be held at a meeting to honour his memory. This should become the rule. And this practice should also be introduced among the people. When someone dies in a village, let a meeting be held in his memory. In this way, by expressing our sorrow, we will be serving to unite all the people.

Discarded